Awakening of a Soldier

ISBN: 979-8-9885303-6-7

Published in United States of America

Published by

Awakening of a Soldier

F.O.I. Style

By

JAMES KENNETH WARD

Published by: O'lemon & Underwood Publishing 379 North Oates Street P. O. Box 95 Dothan, Alabama 36302

Preface

Dive into the rare novel, "The Awakening of a Soldier," an exceptional literary work that takes you on a mesmerizing journey through the depths of America's racial divide and the fight against drug issues – some argue, fueled by government conspiracies but now, have spread to mainstream America. Set in the turbulent 1980s and early 1990s, this captivating novel unfolds during an era when redlining marginalized impoverished communities in the segregated South. Banks labeled these areas as "hazardous," making them ineligible for loans. Witness the resilient spirit of Baptist Bottom, a strong community nestled in the lively city of Dothan, Alabama – widely renowned as the Peanut Capital of the world - as the novel navigates through these challenging times marked by the ongoing impact of desperation and despair.

Baptist Bottom, once a thriving neighborhood that owes its name to the imposing red-brick First Baptist Church at its core, pulses with life and history. Surrounding the church, you'll find McRae homes, a government project built to provide housing for the community, while the Hawk-Houston Boy's

Club stands proudly at its front. The streets of Baptist Bottom were lined with bustling businesses, seamlessly weaving the neighborhood's legacy into the very fabric of southern Alabama's narrative.

In this spirited community, iconic performers such as Marvin Gaye, B.B. King, Clarence Carter, Bobby Womack, Tyrone Davis, James Brown, and Tina Turner once graced the stage, showcasing their talents and leaving a lasting impression on the residents. Little Lois and the Caprees were equally mesmerizing, charming everyone with their harmonious singing, energetic dancing, and delightful entertainment. The rhythmic melodies of Blues and Soul music emanated from the iconic Citizen Club on North Lena Street, situated across from the housing projects, while around the corner, the Capri Club's vibrant mix of R&B and Pop filled the nights with jubilant energy. In Baptist Bottom, social life thrived, providing a sanctuary where residents could dance, revel in their freedom, and forge lasting connections.

Yet, despite the indomitable spirit that pulsated through the community, the inhabitants of Baptist Bottom faced their fair share of adversity. Like the tragic tales of Greenwood's "Black Wall Street" in Oklahoma, Baptist Bottom, too, experienced the devastating consequences of years of oppressive governmental policies. As the pipeline to imprisonment flowed, countless thriving businesses were reduced to ashes, their dreams shattered by a cycle of nightmares.

"The Awakening of a Soldier" weaves together the stories of characters determined to rise above poverty's chains and defy the attempts to silence their voices. It is a poignant exploration of the resilience, courage, and unwavering spirit that thrived amidst the harshest challenges. As you immerse yourself in the pages of this thought-provoking novel, prepare to witness the indelible mark left by Baptist Bottom on the tapestry of history, forever reminding us of the power of community, the pursuit of dreams, and the unbreakable human spirit.

Michael Ray Lemons

Acknowledgments

I extend my heartfelt gratitude to those enduring America's racial divide, facing racism, inequality, and injustice. Your stories and resilience have profoundly inspired this book, serving as a powerful testament to the urgent need for change, understanding, and empathy. Each narrative within these pages reflects your courage and unspoken truths, guiding my learning journey and highlighting voices that often go unheard.

This book is dedicated to you—the brave, the marginalized, and the fighters for justice. It represents a tribute to your indomitable spirit and a call to action for a more inclusive, equitable society. May it resonate as a beacon of hope and a reminder that we must unite in our journey towards equality, ensuring every voice is heard and every story valued. Thank you for inspiring these words and allowing me to continue your stories.

Introduction

In an age of adversity and resolve, there emerged a young man whose story transcends the boundaries of his neighborhood and captivates the hearts of a nation. Growing up as a young black male in America, he faced the familiar challenges that so often define the lives of many. Yet, amidst the hardships, he possessed an extraordinary quality that set him apart - an unwavering desire to carve out a better future for himself and his loved ones.

Bound by the limitations of his surroundings, this kid dared to dream beyond the confines of his humble neighborhood. While others saw only despair and limited opportunities, he glimpsed a life of immense value waiting to be discovered. Day by day, he immersed himself in knowledge, tirelessly seeking a path that would lead him and his family out of the hood once and for all.

Little did he know that his ambition and determination would be the catalyst that catapulted him from Baptist Bottom, a small community nestled within Dothan, Alabama, to the center stage of national television. Baptist Bottom is a symbol of unyielding endurance, a place once marginalized and deemed "hazardous" by banks, rendering it ineligible for loans. Yet resilient black entrepreneurs, craftsmen, merchants, and entertainers banded together to face such obstacles. Their refusal to be silenced fostered dreams that shattered poverty's chains and exhibited their unbeatable spirit in rising above any challenge.

Soon, the name of this young individual would be spoken in the same breath as legendary figures like Martin Luther King Jr. and Malcolm X – iconic African Americans who left an indelible mark on mainstream America. Yet, let us not forget that he is but a young man, with youth, often accompanied by a fair share of mistakes. Through these very mistakes, he would encounter individuals who would connect him with others, ultimately propelling him into the global spotlight for all to witness.

Get ready to embark on an uplifting journey as we delve into the inspiring narrative of this extraordinary young man whose relentless drive for a better future will stand the test of time. Together, let us explore the life-altering power of resilience as we witness how limitless our capabilities can be when we dare to dream big.

Table of Contents

CHAPTER ONE

Choices and Consequences: Nado's Dilemma

Nado observed the men engaging in their daily routine - dealing and consuming drugs. He had always refused to partake, as it contradicted his core values. Raised by a single mother whom his drug-addicted father had abandoned, Nado was shielded from the harsh realities of their neighborhood. Witnessing his mother's constant exhaustion and occasional tears, he vowed to care for her when he was older, seeing her as an unwavering pillar of strength. He blamed his absent father for their struggles, acknowledging the sacrifices his mother made to fulfill both parental roles. Despite her reassurances, Nado remained steadfast in his mission to return the love and support she had selflessly provided for him and his sister, knowing the path he needed to take and the actions necessary to achieve this goal.

Time and again, Nado had received job offers from this man, yet he always declined. The position seemed like a dream come true for underprivileged youth in the neighborhood but without medical insurance and no taxes taken out. Despite this, Nado couldn't help but resent the man.

The man was well-acquainted with Nado, having done his research. He recognized the immense value Nado could bring to his operation. Conversely, Nado was also aware of his potential worth to the man's business and knew he could leverage that knowledge for personal gain. Today marked the beginning of his foray into the ruthless adult world – where only the strongest would survive.

"What's up, Youngblood?" Kong greeted Nado with a grin, perched on his sleek Gold 500 Mercedes Benz. A notorious figure in the underworld, King Kong hailed from Queens, New York. He had relocated to evade the relentless pursuit of federal agents hot on his trail. He quickly fell in love with the serene new location that still held a demand for his services. Kong took great pride in his appearance and self-image as he continued building his empire.

Today, he sported a dark grey Gahanna Pinstripe Suit, which was set off by a pair of grey shoes. On his wrist, Kong wore a diamond-studded 24 Karat Gold Rolex watch. On his finger, he sported a huge nugget ring covered with diamonds. He had the cheddar and made it known. Kong was running low on his supply, and he needed a runner soon. Maybe today would be his lucky day.

Nado was simply on his way to meet up with his friends when Kong approached him. "You seem to have a lot on your mind, Youngblood," Kong stated, hoping he had piqued Nado's interest with their earlier conversation. "I've got grand plans for you. You could go places and see things most people only catch on TV. Escape this place and provide a better life for your mother and sister - no more working for those white folks."

Kong was prepared to list more reasons for Nado to join him, but Nado interrupted first.

Curious, Nado asked, "So, what do I get if I try my hand at it?" Kong smirked, knowing he'd won his interest. "Got a license, kid?" he inquired. "Of course," Nado replied confidently. "Then your first gig earns you 50 stacks if you're in," he offered. Nado nearly choked in disbelief. Fifty thousand dollars? Nado wanted to scream, "What's the catch?" but he managed to keep his cool.

"All you need to do is drive a car to Queens and bring another one back," Kong explained. "Easiest money you'll ever make. And there's more where that came from. I'll give you some product and a place to run your game." At that moment, Nado was sold.

"Let me discuss this with my crew, and I'll get back to you early tomorrow with my decision," Nado said. "Alright, Youngblood. See you then," Kong replied. As Nado walked away, Kong observed him, unable to read his thoughts like he could with others. Had Kong seen the massive smirk on Nado's face, he'd have known that he had triumphed once more. With that, Kong hopped into his car and drove off.

As Nado walked, he began to wonder if he was making the right choice. Could three guys who had never touched as much as a joint handle what was about to happen?

Just as swiftly as the idea had entered his mind, it vanished. Nado was certain that if anyone could pull it off, it would be him and his partners. His crew was a force to be reckoned with, never backing down from anyone. Lil Boot had the stature and strength of a pit bull, while JT Dollar was tall and lean. Nado chuckled, thinking about how they offered their challengers a choice between the two of them to fight – people always chose JT Dollar, which was a huge mistake. Like a Mack Truck engine, both JT and Lil Boot were formidable opponents. Nado smiled as he watched his partners leap into action, sprinting towards him from the porch.

"You've got to have some great news for us, right?" JT asked excitedly. "It's huge. Seriously huge. Listen up - we need to drive a car to Queens and then return with another car. We'll earn 50 stacks just by doing that." Nado responded. "50 grand for driving? What are we waiting for?" JT exclaimed.

"Yeah, let's get going. But there's more, fellas." Nado continued, "Kong said we could make a lot more cash in the future. He's offering to supply me with something and provide a place for it, too. This is the opportunity we've been waiting for – our chance to get our loved ones out of this terrible situation. What do you guys think?" JT didn't hesitate.

"We know that the car we'll be returning with will be loaded with illegal drugs, but it's a risk worth taking. I'm in. How about you, Lil Boot?" Lil Boot confidently replied, "You know I'm always rolling with my boys!" Both JT and Lil Boot then turned to Nado, waiting for his reaction.

"Alright, we're all in agreement," declared Nado. They hung out for a while longer, discussing how they'd spend a bit of their earnings. "I should head home and check on Mom. I'll catch up with you guys early tomorrow. And if Kong needs us, I'll let him know that my team is either all in or all out. Take care," Nado concluded.

"Hey, baby, where have you been all night?" asked Nado's mom as he approached her. He gave her a hug and kissed her cheek. "I was just with JT and Lil Boot. I've been thinking a lot lately. Wouldn't it be great to move out of these projects?" Nado wondered aloud. His mom realized this was the second day in a row they'd had this discussion, and she didn't want to face the truth of where it might be going.

"Mama, I've always admired how you could've made life so much easier for yourself," Nado continued, hesitating briefly as the next part was difficult to say. "Especially after Dad left and why you didn't consider having me and Necy adopted." At this, Mrs. Nell sprang to her feet.

"Don't ever say that, baby! I've never thought about giving you two up to anyone. I would have worked five jobs, if necessary," she declared, taking Nado's hand in hers. "I love you and your sister dearly; never forget that," she added earnestly.

"I understand, Mama. I found a job, and sometimes I might work late or even all night. Please don't worry about me; I'll be fine," said Nado. "What kind of job is it?" she inquired. Nado hesitated for a moment.

"I can't lie to you. I need to do what's necessary so you don't work yourself to death." Mrs. Nell knew what Nado was implying, and she knew that there was nothing that she could say to change his mind. All she could do was pray for his safety. As Nado left, he couldn't bear to see her disappointment. She watched him go and whispered, "God, please protect my child." Wiping away tears, she stared at the empty doorway.

As Nado walked towards the coffee shop, he imagined the better life he could provide his family if their plan succeeded. He didn't intend to deal drugs forever—just long enough to escape the neighborhood.

Approaching the café, he thought about what he wanted to say. Upon entering and seeing only a few customers—including Kong—he greeted him. "Hey, Youngblood! Have something to eat," said Kong warmly. Nado joined him at his table. "You're early today, aren't you?" Kong remarked.

Accepting the offer, Nado excitedly said, "I'm in!" The waiter approached their table, momentarily halting the conversation between Kong and Nado. "What can I get you, young man?" the waiter inquired. "A Coke, please," Nado replied. Once the waiter left, they continued their discussion. "When do you want to go on your trip, Youngblood?" Kong asked. "As soon as possible," Nado responded. Smiling, Kong said, "I've already arranged a car for you."

Feeling eager, Nado declared, "I'm ready to hit the road tonight if that's okay with you." Kong nodded and instructed him to return in an hour, promising he would have directions and contact information for the people who would meet him in Queens.

When the waiter returned with Nado's Coke, he quickly drank it before leaving to prepare for his upcoming adventure. He headed towards a phone booth and dialed his friends to arrange a meetup at the apartments. After hanging up, Nado returned to the café with anticipation for what awaited him on this exciting trip.

"I'm all set to go, Kong," Nado declared. "I appreciate your enthusiasm, Youngblood. Here are the directions and contact details. If you feel tired upon arrival, book a room and catch some sleep. It's crucial not to take any unnecessary risks. If the speed limit is 70 MPH, stick to 65. Don't ever exceed it. I run a highly serious business, and there's no room for mistakes," Kong advised.

Nado grasped the importance of Kong's words. In the parking lot, you'll find an inconspicuous green Ford Taurus with a missing front passenger hubcap. Inside the glove compartment await two envelopes: one containing $1,000 for gas, food, and lodging if needed; the other holding 25 stacks as half your payment. You'll receive the remaining half after your return. "Is that fair to you, Youngblood?" Kong inquired.

"Yes, that's acceptable. So, I'll get the rest upon my return?" Nado questioned. Kong replied assuredly, "The moment you hand over the car keys to me, I'll provide you with the remaining 25 stacks."

Kong dug into his pocket and revealed a set of keys. As Nado reached for the keys, Kong gripped them firmly, looked intently into Nado's eyes, and said, "I'm entrusting you with valuable cargo, Youngblood. Don't disappoint me." Nado grinned. "You can count on me," he replied. Kong nodded and released the keys.

"Safe travels, Youngblood," Kong called out. As Nado walked away, Kong watched him with pride, seeing a young man full of confidence. He knew he'd found the right person for the job.

JT and Lil Boot waited in the parking lot for Nado. Without speaking, he strode past them and headed straight for the car. Just as Kong had promised, there were two envelopes inside. Eagerly, Nado ripped open the thicker one.

"This shit is real, my nigga," Nado announced as he fanned out the hundred-dollar bills. He peeled off five stacks and handed them to Lil Boot. "We'll get the rest when we return." Then, without another word: "I'll be right back." Nado disappeared upstairs, leaving his companions to count their newfound riches.

As Nado pushed the door open, he found his mother sitting at the kitchen table, deep in thought. Approaching her, he planted a tender kiss on her forehead and asked how she was feeling. "I'm fine, baby," she replied. "I was just thinking about you." Her eyes filled with tears as she gazed at her son.

Nado reassured her, "I've got something that'll help us, mama. Just listen." He pulled an envelope from his pocket. "We'll leave the Projects, no matter what it takes." He kissed her cheek and went to his room, returning with a small duffel bag. "I need to go now but will be back tomorrow. Use whatever's in the envelope as needed." Unable to see his mother cry any longer, he hugged her and told her he loved her before making his exit.

"I love you too," she whispered, but Nado didn't hear. Her voice trailed off as they sped away from the parking area. Unbeknownst to him, Mrs. Nell stood near the window, now facing two problems. She'd already sent Necy to live with relatives since she'd started associating with a troublesome crowd.

She knew without a doubt that she had raised her kids right. She closed her eyes and said a prayer. "Keep my children in your right hand." She opened her eyes just in time to see the tail lights disappear out of sight.

———

CHAPTER TWO

The Road to Queens: Challenges and Decisions

It was time for Nado and his friends to hit the road. Cruising along Route 95, they played a Scarface CD and enjoyed their time together. Eventually, Nado realized he was the only one still chaunting out the tunes. He glanced at his friends and grinned; even though they were making good progress, there was still a long way to go. They needed to refuel, so Nado stopped at a gas station. The sudden slamming of the car door jolted Lil Boot and JT awake.

"Groggy, huh? We're already halfway there!" announced Nado as his friends stumbled out of the car to use the restroom and grab some snacks. When they returned, they caught Nado mid-yawn.

"Hey man, want me to take over driving for a bit?" offered Lil Boot. "Nah, I got this," replied Nado. "I just want to get there and back home soon."

As they approached Queens, Nado observed a decrease in the number of white people around. Individuals gathered everywhere, with many just lingering on corners, sipping their drinks. There were people pushing shopping carts, scavenging through dumpsters, and lying on cardboard boxes.

"Look at all those people," JT remarked. "I've never seen so many just hanging out like that." Nado pulled into a service station and took out the phone numbers. Suddenly, there was a knock on the window. He looked up to see a thin woman with three small children clinging to her legs. "Sir, could you spare some change for me to buy food for my kids?" she inquired.

Lil Boot angrily replied, "Back off!" Yet Nado interrupted him, saying, "Wait a second, Lil Boot." He reached into his pocket, pulled out a $20 bill, lowered the window, and handed it over to the woman. She grabbed the money and hurried off, with the children nearly being dragged behind her. Nado observed them entering the store.

Shortly after, they left the store, holding just a single bag of potato chips. Nado observed as the woman approached a man wearing gold chains, handing him her leftover cash. The man then gave her something from a bag, and she took out a pipe to use as her kids fought over the chips.

"I should knock that pipe straight out of her mouth," muttered Lil Boot, but Nado simply shook his head. He suddenly remembered he'd made a call.

"Hello? Apologies for the delay. We're here," Nado spoke into the phone. The voice on the other end responded, "Sorry, this is Freeman Realty. I'm the one who called you earlier about the house on Taurus Lane. Would you like to see it now?"

Cautiously, Nado replied, "Yes, I would like to view it. However, I'm not sure how to find your office. I'm currently at a gas station near Martin Luther King Blvd and Chilton." The voice assured Nado that someone would arrive shortly.

After 15 minutes, an old car pulled up next to them. As they left the area, Nado couldn't help but stare at the lifeless expressions of those around him.

"Can you believe that Shit?" Nado questioned. "They choose to live like that." He felt grateful for his mother and couldn't help but wonder if his father could have been one of those desolate souls lingering on the streets.

Nado's thoughts snapped back to reality as the car he trailed entered a garage parking lot. No words were exchanged, just firm handshakes. The man pointed towards a worn-out Ford LTD and declared, "There is your house." Nado was confused, and his puzzled expression was evident and the man quickly added, "The exterior may need some touch-ups, but the interior is in perfect condition and flawless. How long do you plan to stay in town?"

Nado replied, "We'll grab some food, find a room, and leave around noon tomorrow." The man nodded and placed three ticket stubs onto the LTD's dashboard. "This is for you if the cops stop you – Lakers versus Knicks from last night's game. Stay safe." They shook hands again before the man climbed into his car and drove off.

However, Nado hadn't been entirely honest with him. While they did plan to eat, they had no intention of staying in New York overnight. Nado refused to make himself an easy target for anyone. "This is it, Fellas. Now, all we have to do is get home. Are You guys ready?" Nado asked.

"Yeah, ready to eat," JT exclaimed. They all laugh. Moments later, they found themselves at KFC. Once finished indulging, they set off for the interstate. Despite a few misguided turns costing Nado an hour of driving, they were eventually back on track. That is, until flashing blue lights appeared in Nado's rearview mirror.

"Stay calm; we've got company," Nado remarked, shivering as the police car pulled up behind them. Visions of his mother's face filled his mind while observing the two officers approaching their car. One headed towards Nado while the other stood by the back passenger's side with a hand resting on his weapon. The officer tapped on Nado's window.

Nado rolled down the window and greeted him with a smile. "Good evening, sir," said the officer, his expression stoic. Using a flashlight to illuminate Nado's face, he requested, "May I see your license, please?"

"Of course, sir," Nado replied. Carefully removing his wallet from his back pocket while keeping it visible, he retrieved his license and handed it over to the officer.

"Stay put, Sir," the officer replied, promptly calling in the number. In five minutes, he returned with news of a livestock truck that had overturned further up the road, cautioning them about loose animals. Curiously, he asked what are you boys doing way up here? "Came up here to catch Kobe," Nado replied, producing some old ticket stubs from the dashboard. The officer wished them safe travels and handed Nado his license before returning to his vehicle. Relieved, Lil Boot expressed his gladness that they hadn't been questioned about the game as they all laughed, and Nado pulled away.

"Did you notice that huge guy behind our car?" JT nervously asked. "Hard not to," Lil Boot retorted. They had narrowly escaped trouble with the law; now, their focus was getting home.

Kong received a call from the guy from Freedman Realty updating him on the exchange. "They like the house; they were hungry and likely asleep now. I'm planning on seeing them at noon tomorrow." Kong just listens intently without uttering a word, solely interested in confirming the details of the exchange.

"I think my phone's malfunctioning; I can't hear anything you're saying. Are you still there?" After ten seconds of silence, the caller repeated "hello" "hello" – a covert way of saying 'take care my friends' – before hanging up.

They were on top of their game, but so was the opposing team. They had uncovered Kong's associates and tapped all their phones. Eager to hear Kong's voice, they only intercepted conversations about buying and selling houses. Meanwhile, they patiently awaited the next call, hoping it would be from Kong himself.

Finally, they heard, "Welcome to Atlanta Georgia." In just a few hours, everything would come to a resolution. JT and Lil Boot remained alert while Nado grew tired.

"I'm gonna throw away all the shit I have and buy me all new shit, said Lil Boot. JT Dollar chimed in, "I'm curious to see what Kong will give us."

JT continued, "I hope he doesn't mess around with the rest of the money. If he does, I won't hesitate to kick his ass. Yeah, let's just see what he's talking about, fellas," Nado replied, "I don't think he'll bullshit us."

"How much are we transporting, Nado? Should we take this apart with a crowbar to see what's inside?" asked JT. Nado responded cautiously, "Hold on. If we mess with this car, we may have no choice but to kill Kong for real."

"Think about this, Nado – if he's got 50 stacks lying around, there must be plenty more where that came from," remarked Lil Boot. Imagining their future as the dominant players in town, Nado and JT shared a laugh. "If all goes according to plan, we'll be the top dogs around here soon enough. We just need to play by the rules for now and see if Kong gives us his support. I just hope we're prepared," Nado mused with anticipation. As he parked in the project lot, Nado glanced up to see a familiar face: Mrs. Nells, her expression brightening at the sight of her loved one.

Sensing his mother's relief as they embraced, Nado reassured her, "Don't worry, Mom – everything's alright. I told you I'd be back. You really think my brothers would let anything happen to me?" He added, "I'm just going to step out for a moment; I'll be right back." Each of them gave Mrs. Nell a kiss before departing together.

"Mrs. Nell watched with relief as they walked away; her child, safe and unharmed, had returned. He had never disappointed her, and she knew he wouldn't start now."

As Nado made his way back, he couldn't help but notice the quaint little coffee shop where he spotted Kong's car. Eager to catch him before he slipped away, Nado wanted to avoid being liable for the car overnight and, more importantly, secure the rest of his payment. Neither Lil Boot nor JT Dollar had ever met Kong personally, but they were certainly familiar with his face and occupation.

Upon entering the coffee shop, they immediately caught sight of Kong's surprised expression. "Full of surprises, Youngblood! I wasn't expecting to see you until tomorrow. Heard you were exhausted," said Kong, curious about their early appearance. Nado didn't feel like chatting; instead, he pulled out the car keys and handed them over. "And who are these two Youngbloods?" Kong inquired.

"They're my partners, JT and Lil Boot," Nado replied. Neither spoke or offered their hand; they just nodded and left it at that. They were waiting on Kong to tremble with the stacks so that they could kick him out of that expensive ass suit he had on.

"Feeling a little drained, huh? It's been quite a day," Nado remarked. Kong gestured for Nado to join him outside. "You impressed me today, Youngblood," Kong praised as he disabled his car alarm, reached in, and withdrew a hefty envelope. "Here's the full amount I promised. Feel free to count it now, but I assure you it's all here. We'll discuss our remaining business tomorrow morning—just come see me."

Nado accepted the envelope with a nod, then strolled away. Kong smirked to himself, thinking about the perfect place for Nado and his crew. They headed towards Lil Boots' house since it was the nearest among the three partners' residences. Once settled indoors, Nado addressed his companions.

"We have accomplished the first part of what we set out to do. We're about to step into an entirely new level of the game tomorrow—I hope we're prepared," cautioned Nado. He opened the envelope, handing five stacks each to his partners before continuing, "I have to head home and rest up. Let's meet at my place around eight in the morning; we can go see Kong together."

Upon reaching the door, Nado deftly inserted his key and stepped inside. To his surprise, he found his mother asleep at the kitchen table, her head resting on its surface. For a brief moment, he admired the incredible woman who had sacrificed so much to ensure a bright future for him and his sister. Approaching her gently, Nado laid his head on her raven hair and stroked it tenderly.

"Mama, time to wake up," he softly whispered. Gradually, Mrs. Nell's heavy eyes opened, and upon seeing Nado, a warm smile spread across her face. "Hey there, sweetie. Mama's just so exhausted." "Why don't you go to bed, and we can chat tomorrow?" suggested Nado. "Alright, honey. See you in the morning," she replied. With a loving kiss on his forehead, Mrs. Nell wearily made her way down the hall to her bedroom.

A few minutes later, as Nado prepared for bed himself, he passed by his mother's room and noticed her sprawled across the bed, shoes still on. In that instant, he made a solemn promise never to let his mother experience such fatigue and weariness again. If she ever worked another day in her life, it would be because she wanted to, not because she had to. Nado walked to his room and sat down to take off his shoes.

"Rise and shine, buddy. Time for the mall!" Lil Boot and JT Dollar were up with the sun. Nado's eyes sluggishly opened to see his two friends peering down at him. "What time is it?" he inquired groggily. "Time to get going," Lil Boot replied, "You must've been tired. Look like you slept ready to roll. You even slept with your shoes on!" Nado sat up, and chuckling at the thought of his mother and laughed.

"I need a quick shower, then I'm good to go," Nado announced as he dashed off to the bathroom. In just a few minutes, he emerged and began getting dressed. "Anyone else hungry? What's for breakfast?"

"Sausage, egg, and cheese Mcgriddle," shouted Lil Boot. "I'll have pancakes and coffee," said JT. "I'll be right down in a minute. I got to let Mom know where I'm going."

Nado approached Mrs. Nell's room and gave a gentle knock. "Mom, I'm heading out for some food with JT and Boot. Need anything?" he asked. "No, honey, I'm good. I'll just be going to the store for a few items," she replied.

"Alright, see you later then," Nado said with a warm smile. "Take care, baby," she responded. Nado then exited the house and joined his friends outside.

Upon entering McDonald's, the cheerful employee greeted them excitedly, "Welcome to McDonald's. Can I take your order, please?" Nado found himself captivated by the cashier's friendly demeanor and caught himself staring at her name tag - Azurie. While Nado was momentarily distracted, JT nudged him out of the way and placed his order. "I'll have some pancakes, a large coffee, and two sausage egg and cheese McGriddles with a large orange juice."

Still motionless, Nado continued observing Azurie as she took down JT and Lil Boot's orders with her contagious smile. Noticing his fixation, she asked about their quiet companion: "What would your friend like?" To which JT jokingly replied about Nado's uncharacteristic silence, "Oh, you mean Mr. Speechless over there?"

Finally shaking off his momentary daze, Nado squeaked out his order: "I'll have what they're having!" After paying for their meals, Nado waited as his friends left. "I'm sorry, um." "Azurie," she replied, introducing herself. Once they got their food, Nado and his companions turned to leave. He couldn't help but wonder why he was apologizing. Suddenly, chaos erupted at the front counter.

"What's with my order? It's always messed up!" Nado observed as an unruly man, argued with Azurie. Calmly, she assured him, "No problem, sir. We'll make it right." As Nado watched, Azurie dug into her pocket and handed the man a ten-dollar bill along with a complimentary breakfast. Little did he know that this man pulled the same stunt twice a week, expecting Azurie's generous response.

Although aware of the man's tricks, Azurie had a soft spot for him. She often saw him scavenging through trash cans and wearing the same clothes. But she didn't mind losing $20 a week because she knew he needed it more than her. With a smile on her face, she witnessed the grumbling man exit the establishment.

Nado sneaked another look at Azurie as he exited, but she was too occupied with taking orders to notice his gaze. "C'mon, get in the car! What on earth happened to you in there? They asked you what you wanted to eat, and you just froze. She must be stunning," said Lil Boot. Laughing, he added, "JT, if my Nigga froze like that, she's got to be something special."

"It wasn't like that, man. I was just deep in thought," Nado defended himself. Lil Boot and JT exchanged amused smiles.

"How'd you manage to borrow your uncle's car, JT?" Nado inquired. "I paid him $50 and said I had a hot date." As they pulled out of the parking lot, Nado unsuccessfully attempted another glimpse of Azurie, but her image was already etched into his memory. When they hit the mall, it was game on. They visited every store and bought all the items they had desired.

For once, they didn't have to worry about prices. Once their shopping spree concluded, it was time for the arcade. But Nado's thoughts lingered elsewhere.

"Guys, I'll be right back. I just need to check something out," Nado stated. He strolled towards D&S, searching for the perfect gift for his mother. A store assistant approached him and asked if he needed help. "Yes, ma'am. I'm looking for a beautiful dress for my mom," Nado responded, handing her a note with his mother's dress and shoe sizes.

Within five minutes, the assistant returned with an exquisite Dolce & Gabbana dress and matching lavender Prada ostrich skin shoes—the most stunning ensemble Nado had ever laid eyes on. The $950 price tag was irrelevant; he wanted his mom to have an unforgettable evening.

After paying, Nado continued his shopping spree at Bailey's Jewelry Store, where he chose a lovely V-shaped herringbone necklace and bracelet set for $1100. Arms overflowing with presents, he clumsily returned to the game room.

"Ready to head out?" Nado asked his friends. Lil Boot let out a frustrated expletive as his last ship exploded in their game.

Altogether, the trio had acquired enough clothes from every store in the mall to consider their shopping session a success.

Brands like Sean John, Rocawear, Phat Farm, Baby Phat, Guess, Polo, and Nautica lined the car, accompanied by a variety of shoes - T-mac 3, Adidas, Puma, And 1, Lugs, and naturally, Jordans.

"JT, let's stop here," Nado suggested. He swiftly entered the tuxedo store and emerged within 10 minutes. "Where to now?" JT inquired.

"Let's visit Kong," Nado replied. Soon after, they arrived at the little coffee shop. "Let's head in," Nado urged.

"Hey there, Youngblood!" Kong greeted them. "Just seeing if Johnny is around," Nado replied. Kong nodded knowingly. "Tell him we'll be here tomorrow morning at 8 in the morning if you see him." "Will do. Take care, Youngblood," responded Kong.

As they started walking back to their car, Nado requested that he be dropped back home as he had a date planned. "Who's the lucky one?" Lil Boot asked curiously. "Nunna."

"Nunna, who?" inquired Lil Boot again. JT and Nado laughed in unison before saying together: "Nunna, your nosy business." "Man, forget you guys!" Lil Boot jokingly scoffed.

—

CHAPTER THREE

Turning Points: Nado's Crossroads

JT parked the car, and Nado quickly gathered his belongings. "Catch you later," he said before disappearing. Once inside his home, he made the most of his mother's absence. He carefully laid out the dress on her bed and positioned the shoes at the foot of it. Double-checking his reservations over the phone, Nado then stowed away the items he'd picked up at the mall for himself. Exhausted, he finally allowed himself a few hours of rest, but as he drifted off to sleep, he realized he'd forgotten the name of that stunning girl he longed to see again.

His mother's voice jolted Nado awake. "Nado, baby? Where did this dress and these shoes come from?" asked Mrs. Nell.

"I bought them for you, Mama," Nado replied. But she was perplexed and touched. "You didn't need to spend your money on me, baby. How much was it?" inquired Mrs. Nell.

"Mama, please just listen to me. I don't want you worrying about prices when it comes to gifts from me. You've earned the right to not care about that. So, do you like the outfit and shoes?" Nado inquired.

"Absolutely, sweetheart, they're stunning. I'll probably wear them to church on Sunday; this dress seems too lovely not to be worn," Mrs. Nell replied, holding the dress against herself and strolling towards the mirror. Her radiant smile made Nado yearn to gift her endless dresses if it meant seeing that beautiful expression forever.

"Well, I hate to be a buzz kill, Mom, but you won't be wearing it on Sunday," Nado remarked. He watched his mother's smile fade momentarily. "That's because you're wearing it tonight! We have a six o'clock date together – no questions about the destination allowed," he declared playfully. Mrs. Nell placed the dress on the bed and walked over to embrace Nado.

"Now, if you keep lingering here, your legs might not hold up for our evening plans," teased Nado. "Don't count on that, dear. I wouldn't dare miss this date for anything in the world," she confidently asserted. By 5:30 pm, both were dressed impeccably and ready for their mysterious outing.

"You look stunning, Mom," Nado complimented. "So do you, Nado," she replied. "But it feels like something's missing. Doesn't the dress seem like something is missing, Mom? Why don't you take a look in the mirror?" suggested Nado. Mrs. Nell went to the mirror and stared at the dress. "Could you have left it on the dresser?" Without giving it much thought, she glanced down and then looked back up at the mirror. Nado had appeared behind her, holding up a thick, V-shaped herringbone necklace. Mrs. Nell was speechless, with her hand covering her mouth. Her son then tenderly placed the necklace around her neck and fastened a bracelet on her wrist. "If that gorgeous lady in the mirror wasn't my mom, I'd ask her to marry me," Nado teased, causing his mother to blush.

Suddenly, there was a knock on the door. "Who is it?" called out Mrs. Nell. "I'd like to speak with the lady of the house, please." Curious, Mrs. Nell opened the door and asked, "Are you looking for me?"

"Yes, I am," said the man as he bent down to pick up the box of roses. "I suppose it's quite fitting – beautiful roses for a beautiful lady." He handed the box to Mrs. Nell. "Your ride is waiting, ma'am." Mrs. Nell was puzzled, having never experienced such treatment.

"Put your flowers away, mama. The man is waiting for you." Mrs. Nell quickly placed the roses on the kitchen table and dashed back to the front door. Nado approached his mom and slipped his arm through hers. "Shall we go?"

Outside, a massive crowd had assembled. It wasn't every day that a limo appeared in the project. Even before Mrs. Nell stepped outside, she could hear the commotion. Suddenly, someone cried out, "That's who they're here for!" All eyes turned to Nado and Mrs. Nell.

"Check out that dress," remarked a bystander. "I saw the same one at D & S!" Hearing them discuss her gown made Mrs. Nell feel exceptional. She anticipated their next comment about her outfit: that it cost a staggering $2,500. Mrs. Nell couldn't believe it – oh my God!

Exuding the aura of royalty, she confidently held her head high. Suddenly, everything clicked - the luxurious pearl-white limousine parked nearby, with the flower-giver standing next to it, holding the door open. As they journeyed, Nado gazed at the exhilarating scene, his mother's face in awe.

Upon arrival, the driver held the door for Nado and Mrs. Nell as they stepped out. Surrounded by fancy cars and a "Top of the World" sign, Mrs. Nell was stunned by their destination - a place only frequented by the wealthiest of people. As Nado offered his arm, she beamed and linked hers with his.

Arm in arm, they entered the rooftop elevator. With all eyes on them, they gracefully made their way to their table. Mrs. Nell marveled at the breathtaking location, further enchanted by it as their drinks were ordered. Throughout the night, numerous guests praised her stunning appearance at their table.

As their drinks arrived, Nado signaled the waiter that they were prepared to order their meal. Later, Nado danced with the most beautiful woman in the room. While they twirled around the dance floor, Mrs. Nell reminisced about how her late husband used to take her dancing, seeing so much of him in Nado. Mid-dance, dinner made its way to the table.

"Did you have fun tonight, Mom?" asked Nado. Mrs. Nell replied, "Darling, besides giving birth to you and your sister, this has been the happiest day of my life." After dinner, they took the elevator down and returned to their awaiting limousine. Upon arriving back at their apartment, Nado noticed his mother staring at her reflection in the mirror. Catching his gaze, she felt embarrassed.

"Thank you for tonight's lovely experience," she said softly. "Trust me, Mom – this is just a glimpse of the good times ahead," assured Nado. "Now, if you don't have plans for us elsewhere, I'm going to change out of these clothes." With that, Nado headed to his room.

From that moment, he knew he would never see his mother without again. Nado had finally caught up on sleep and was up early, energized for the next part of their mission. He grabbed his phone and called his partners.

"Are you guys ready to roll?" Nado asked. "We're ready dawg. Just wait until you see what Lil Boot done got. Them white folks gone have a field day with this nigga," JT replied.

"What are you guys waiting for? Well, come and scoop me. I'll be waiting downstairs," Nado said as he hung up and walked out the door. Within five minutes, a white Pontiac Parisienne pulled up next to him. "Lil Boot's limo, at your service!" Lil Boot announced with a grin. JT hopped out and ceremoniously opened the back door for Nado.

"This is tight, Lil Boot. How did you find it?" Nado inquired. Lil Boot chuckled, "There was this old man with it sitting in his yard. When I asked if it was for sale, he said no initially. But that changed when I showed him that I was stacked." Lil Boot smiled.

"Nado excitedly announced, "My boy got all new everything! I came by your crib last night to show you, but nobody answered. "Let's head to Micky D's, and I want to check something." Said Nado. The guys chuckled and teased him about his intentions. Nado admitted his previous encounter was flawed, but he remained confident.

As they pulled into the parking lot, Nado hopped out of the car, stating, "Be right back," while smoothing his shirt. Entering the restaurant, he scanned the area for the cashier whom he had come to see. Not finding her, he asked a nearby employee. "Excuse me," said Nado. I'm looking for a young lady who usually works the cash register.

Pausing for a moment, the girl answered, "Azurie? She's off today. She goes to the mosque on her days off. Maybe she's home now? But I don't know where she lives. You could find her at the mosque on Sunset Blvd by 2 PM. Are you Muslim?"

"No, I'm not Muslim," Nado replied. "But if I don't get to see her, can you tell her Nado stopped by?"

"Alright, guys, let's get this done," said Nado confidently. Just as expected, Kong was present. Lil Boot parked the car, and they watched as Kong approached them. "What's up, Youngbloods?" asked Kong. "We need to take a drive. You're riding with me so we can have a chat," he continued. Nado climbed into the car with Kong while Lil Boot and JT stayed behind, waiting for them to leave. "I don't trust that punk ass nigga. Something's off about him," JT confided in Lil Boot.

Kong's car was like something from a luxury magazine – decked with a TV, CD player, minibar, and much more. As Nado admired his surroundings, Kong posed a question: "Do you know anything about this business?" Nado considered lying but ultimately decided that honesty was the best policy if he needed any help. "No, I don't, but I'm willing to learn," he replied. "That's good to hear; your honesty is appreciated. I'll teach you everything you need to know," assured Kong, checking his rearview mirror in the process. "I have a knack for reading people. Your partner seems quiet on the surface, but there's more than meets the eye."

Nado nodded in agreement. "He should be in charge of handling problems since this line of work can be quite problematic. At times, you'll need to step out of your comfort zone and protect what's important to you."

"Any harm that comes your way mustn't go unanswered," Kong continued. "For every action, there must be an appropriate response. That's where your foot soldiers come in – that's where the other Youngbloods fit into all this. From what I've seen of you guys – you're the brains of the operation and should lead all major decisions, including handling money and the heavyweight. Youngblood Shorty should manage the street soldiers, while Youngblood Slim can supply small weight and make sure your back is covered."

"This is all connected – your main goal is to make money. You must have heard the saying, 'Out-of-town troublemakers get Swiss Cheesed Up.' Ensure that no one else is stepping on your turf, or you and your crew will face consequences." Kong explained to Nado as he drove into a run-down motel.

He parked behind the office and signaled for the others to follow him.

Kong punched in the code, unlocking the door. As it swung open, they saw a man accompanied by two attractive women inside. The room was filled with various items, but Nado's gaze was instantly drawn to six large packages of what appeared to be cocaine.

"Alright, let's get started," announced Kong. "These Youngbloods don't have a clue about cutting, cooking, or bagging, so we're starting from scratch." The man lifted one of the packages. "This here is a kilo – 36 ounces of powder. You could sell it as-is for an average of $700 an ounce, adding up to $25,200."

He continued, "There are 28 grams in an ounce, and each gram fetches around $100. An 8-ball contains 3.5 grams and usually sells for around $200. Breaking down the product into smaller quantities can yield more profit, but it also means dealing with more people and attracting police attention."

"To cut a kilo or 'bird' like this, mix it with 18 ounces of additive. This will boost your profit margins while decreasing potency—but keep in mind that high-quality products sell themselves. If you can move top-tier merchandise quickly enough, the profits will follow."

"Now, let's talk about cooking powder into crack cocaine," said the man as he delved into different methods and ingredients used in the process. As the man demonstrated each step, he began by cooking an ounce of cocaine. After completing the process, he weighed it and then prepared a second batch, adding an ounce of an additive that caused the cocaine to expand. Each mixture resulted in different colors – sometimes white, other times tan, or light pink. Surprisingly, another batch with added chloroform turned the product blue.

Once finished, he weighed the final product, now double its original weight. The man then explained, "What you've just seen is a comparison between quality and quantity. A true smoker would prefer the first ounce because of its superior quality and more intense high. Take, for example, a 16 oz Coke in a plastic bottle – it's tough to drink it all in one go. But if you order a Coke with ice at a restaurant and let it sit until you reach your destination, the ice melts, diluting the drink. You could easily have two in quick succession. The reason? It's not pure Coke anymore; it's watered down. That's exactly what happened here with these two ounces of cocaine – transforming it from its original state."

Nado grasped the man's point entirely. "It'll still sell, of course, but smokers opt for the top-quality stuff if they can find it. You're their fallback option. When people discuss your products, you want them to say, 'They've always got the good stuff.' So, gentlemen, roll up your sleeves and get ready for some work."

"No cut," Nado declared. "Master the technique without any additives." Kong grinned at Nado's choice, and the man complimented him on his wise decision. After giving Lil Boot and JT some useful advice, he stepped back to observe their progress. It wasn't long before they were swiftly producing cookies while the ladies packaged them.

"Excellent job, my friend," Kong praised. He informed the man that his work was complete and handed him a stack of bills, adding, "See you next time." The man signaled to the girls that it was time to go, and they obediently trailed behind him.

With a serious tone, Kong said to them, "Now let's discuss business. I have six birds for you if you can handle them. I expect 12 grand per bird – that's 72 grand in total. Your profit will be considerably more than double what I'm charging you. However, before you splurge on cars, clothes, and jewelry, remember to pay me first. Losing is not an option for my associates. Am I making myself clear, Youngbloods?"

Such words were uncalled for. JT hoped Kong didn't assume they would simply bend to his will. After a pause, JT spoke up. "Listen, man, we'll bring in the money, and you'll get your cut. If you or your crew ever feel like you're losing out because of us, speak up, and we'll handle it."

JT faced Kong with an unyielding expression, the room filled with palpable tension. Both men held each other's gaze, neither one backing down. Eventually, Kong's smile broke the tension as he glanced towards Nado.

"See? I'm rarely wrong," Kong said confidently. Approaching JT, he shook his hand warmly. "I know you'll do well, Youngblood." He then addressed Nado, "Are we in agreement?" As Nado turned towards his crew, each gave an affirming nod. He faced Kong and confirmed with a single word: "Deal." They sealed their partnership with a handshake.

"Well, I guess it's time for me to head back to the coffee shop," said Kong. "After you're done here, swing by, and we'll go for a drive."

Kong couldn't help but grin as he strolled toward his car, feeling confident with brains and brawn on his side. Meanwhile, back in their workspace, the pharmacists were hard at work. JT and Lil Boot prepared rocks while Nado handled the powder.

"Let's see our earnings this time around. Maybe we'll try cutting it and adding vitamin E next time," they thought aloud, considering improvements for future endeavors. "Divide the rocks into nine $10 pieces and pack them in zip-loc bags of tens," JT instructed Lil Boot.

Ounces of crack were also bagged separately. Once everything was laid out, they calculated their earnings and set aside Kong's share before beginning their own count.

They marveled at their hefty profit, each earning over 50 stacks. The partners exchanged high fives and laid out their plan: Lil Boot would handle the smaller deals, working closely with someone dependable on the streets; JT would manage larger transactions and ensure a steady supply. Meanwhile, Nado would control finances and the business end like fronting, big ballers, and stuff like that. No one person will serve anything over a quarter bird by himself.

The group stressed the importance of not appearing weak or vulnerable to competitors and agreed to stand together when necessary. Aware that not every dollar would be made as planned, they remained optimistic about their overall profits. With everything discussed and sorted, it was time for them to clear up their workspace and move forward.

Nado hadn't given much consideration to where he'd store the plethora of drugs, but now it was time to think. With just an hour left before his appointment, he quickly packed everything into a large duffel bag. "I need to drop this off at home. Mom would kill me if she found it," Nado remarked.

"I might have an idea about where we can stash it—let's go and see," suggested Nado as he stepped out of the car and approached the door, nervously inserting the key. Surprisingly, the apartment was still quiet—his mom hadn't returned from church yet. Hurrying to his room, Nado stowed the mysterious duffel bag on a shelf above his hanging clothes—a close call as he heard the front door shut just moments later.

"Nado, are you home?" called his mom. Caught in the act, Nado tried to play it cool. "Yes, ma'am," he replied, emerging from his room. "I was just about to head out on an errand. What took you so long to get back from church today?" he asked curiously.

"I had to go by the bus station. I paid for Necy a ticket to come home tomorrow," Mrs. Nell shared, her voice trailing off as she gazed into the distance. Nado sensed there was more to the story than she was revealing, but he had a critical meeting to attend and couldn't afford to be late. "Mom, can we discuss this later?" Nado inquired. "Sure, honey, we'll chat when you're back," Mrs. Nell responded, observing Nado leave the house.

The stroll to Sunset Blvd. was brief; Nado arrived at the mosque with a singular goal – to speak with Azurie. With only ten minutes to spare, he anxiously scanned the arriving guests from their cars. A nagging urge tempted him to check for Azurie inside, but at last, he spotted her getting out of a car, accompanied by a couple he presumed were her parents.

Azurie glanced upward, immediately noticing Nado's intent gaze upon her. She surmised there could be only one reason for his presence: herself. As Nado observed Azurie engaging with a man and woman, he followed their movement into the mosque before Azurie finally approached him. Intrigued, she examined Nado closely.

"Hello, Azurie. No, it's not a coincidence that I'm here. I tried to find you at work this morning, but you weren't there."

"How did you know where to look for me?" Azurie questioned, suddenly remembering who was working the register that day.

"I'd be putting myself at a disadvantage if I revealed my information source," Nado replied with a grin. Realizing his slyness wasn't enough for her, Azurie asked, "So, why are you visiting me?"

"I had this overwhelming urge to see you. I don't want to take up too much of your time; I just wanted to invite you to a movie or dinner sometime," Nado confessed and felt like a schoolboy under Azurie's scrutiny. "I have a break at 11 tomorrow. We can discuss it more then."

"Let me just say, you are incredibly stunning," Nado complimented. "I wouldn't miss tomorrow for the world." Azurie replied, "Thank you, but I must go, as the service is about to begin." Nado courteously opened the door for her, feeling grateful as he watched her walk down the aisle toward another woman. He then observed a man by the door, who caught his gaze.

"Please forgive me," Nado apologized to the man before leaving with an overwhelming sense of triumph. He had everything he wanted − drugs, money, and now a beautiful woman.

Meeting up with his friends, Nado inquired excitedly, "Guys, are we ready to see Kong? Come on, let's go!" They all hopped into Lil Boot's car and made their way to the little coffee shop where Kong was waiting. Upon arrival, they followed him on the highway toward Roanoke Rapids. As they journeyed together, reflecting on their accomplishments since venturing onto their chosen turf just a year ago − they couldn't help but feel proud.

Reflecting on their first day, they had boldly stood on the street and given away free samples of drugs to make a name for themselves. The following day, sales exploded so much that it left them astonished. They never imagined such a small area could bring in that much cash. A year later, each of them had relocated their families from the troubled neighborhood to beautiful homes.

They also bought numerous cars for themselves and their families. Nado was particularly raking in money since he made deliveries for Kong while Lil Boot and JT focused on operating on the streets. Nado provided his family with a massive two-story house in the suburbs, hoping to protect his sister from the city's temptations.

However, she seemed increasingly attracted to so-called bad boys and thugs. Isolating her and placing Mrs. Nell as her only companion seemed to help bring back the sister he had always known. Nado showered Necy and his mother with countless gifts.

Nado used this as a reason to justify his constant absence from home. When he was around, he'd spend most of his time in the shed near the garage, which housed his mother's red Toyota Camry and his sleek black BMW 740i. Being less extravagant than his associates and making frequent trips to Queens allowed him to amass more wealth.

———

CHAPTER FOUR

Crossroads of Conscience: Nado's Dilemma

One day, Nado was caught off guard when his mom handed him back an unopened envelope containing the money from his first job with Kong. He had a secret stash of over $400,000 hidden in a specially designed compartment within the walls of his cherished shed.

His plan was to quit after three years and, if all went well, become a millionaire sooner. All he needed to do was stay cautious and vigilant. Nado's thoughts drifted back to Azurie and their first dinner date. To impress her, he had bought an extravagant Dolce & Gabbana suit with matching shoes and adorned himself with numerous diamond and gold rings. He could still hear her inquiring about what he did for a living, as if she were right beside him at this very moment.

The question caught him completely off guard, leaving him momentarily speechless. Before he could respond, Azurie said she had enjoyed their evening together but believed it would be their last. She explained that what she wanted in life couldn't be found with someone who didn't share her level of ambition. Nado thought to himself, "I don't need you or your ambitions."

A year later, memories of Azurie still haunted him, just like they had many nights before. He recalled her sorrowful eyes as he walked her to the door that night. Shaking himself back to reality, Nado parked his 740 IE and went to collect the weekly earnings from Lil Boot. He found Lil Boot behind the apartments, arguing with one of the other men.

Nado intervened, "You always seem to have some type of excuse. I don't care about your personal problems. If you don't have my money, then you'll have a problem with me." Lil Boot turned to face Nado.

"It seems like you're having a problem. You know me, homie, there's nothing I can't handle," said Lil Boot with confidence. He strolled over to the apartments and returned a few minutes later, clutching a briefcase. He handed it off to Nado.

"I'll return after I stash this away," Nado muttered to himself, thinking about their fortunate turn of events. He stepped aside to let a man pass by, but the stranger had different plans.

"Hand over the briefcase," the man demanded, brandishing what looked like a gun at Nado. Acting on instinct, Nado raised his hands in surrender, accidentally bumping himself with the briefcase. With no warning, the assailant punched Nado in the stomach, sending him to his knees. As Nado's vision cleared, he looked up to see the man towering over him.

"Give me the briefcase," the man repeated firmly. But then, unexpectedly, he started collapsing to the ground. Confused at first, Nado soon saw the reason for the man's abrupt fall – Lil Boot was furiously pounding and stomping on his head, forcing it into the concrete sidewalk.

Aware of the urgency, Nado quickly intervened for the man's benefit. Summoning all his strength, he pulled Lil Boot back from the unconscious man who had just attempted to rob him. "It's okay, partner. I'm okay," he reassured. Moments later, Nado spotted a police car stealthily entering the parking lot.

Realizing the situation, Nado instantly took action. He grabbed the briefcase and handed it to Lil Boot. "Take this and go now." Without hesitation, Lil Boot snatched up the briefcase and sprinted away as fast as he could. Suddenly, Nado was caught in the glare of a spotlight from the police car.

The scene depicted Nado standing over the still figure of the man Lil Boot had knocked out on the sidewalk. He watched as the car stopped abruptly in front of him, and a large officer wielding a hefty gun emerged from it.

"Freeze! Don't move, or I'll splatter your brains all over the sidewalk," the officer threatened fiercely. Despite his pain, Nado knew that he shouldn't make a single move.

"Slowly raise your hands above your head, and don't stop until you grasp the moon," the officer instructed. Nado lifted his arms, feeling his muscles stretch. "That's far enough, boy. And don't make any sudden moves on me, boy; I'd hate to have to shoot you," the cop said with a grin. "I'd like to see you try and take my gun," the officer added confidently. He then approached the man lying on the ground, shining his flashlight onto his face, making the man's eyelids flutter.

The policeman glanced back at Nado and sighed, "What a shame. If I'd been a bit slower, maybe you could've finished what you started. There would've been one less nigger running around here smoking dope." He ordered Nado, "Place your hands on your head and come towards the car." Moving slowly, Nado approached the vehicle until his knees touched the bumper. "Now, put your hands on the hood." He obeyed, and the officer patted him down before handcuffing him.

Nado had never been more relieved to see police officers arrive. As more of them entered the parking lot, he felt increasingly safe. "Put his ass in the car," an officer commanded. Nado watched as they searched the man on the ground.

People had gathered all around, and a slender black police officer approached the first cop on the scene. Nado overheard their conversation about the incident. "Those stupid niggas never learn, do they, Jim Bob? All they do is rob and kill each other. I'm grateful I didn't get involved in that life," said the black officer. Nado couldn't stand it – there was nothing worse than a self-righteous Black cop trying to prove himself to his white colleagues. Despite this, Nado felt certain that telling the truth would resolve the situation.

In the interrogation room, Nado recounted the events to the officers. However, one of them retorted, "That's nonsense! We have two witnesses who saw you attack and beat up the man while attempting to rob him. Did he try to resist? You mentioned he had a gun; did you hide it before we arrived?" Nado insisted that the man had threatened him with a gun.

The officer continued, "We visited the victim in the hospital. He claims that when he tried to walk past you, you hit him in the face and tried to take something from his pocket. When he tried to stop you, you beat and kicked him until he lost consciousness. A concerned citizen's intervention is what got you caught."

The worried observer turned out to be elderly, partially blind woman who, after hearing a commotion, had seen the silhouette of one man hovering above another. She was unaware that she had witnessed Nado on the ground and his assailant looming over him.

After enduring two weeks of medical care, the injured man was finally discharged from the hospital. His nose and jaw had been broken, he'd lost an eye, and two of his front teeth had been knocked out. On a positive note, Nado's associates were already prepared to post his bail at the jailhouse.

Upon posting bail, the trio headed to a peaceful little eatery for a meal. Lil Boot expressed gratitude to Nado and empathized with his actions: "You didn't have to take the fall for me, Nado. But I get it – he crossed the line, so I had to make sure he paid."

"Don't worry, Lil Boot, you came to my rescue. I should've been more cautious. How'd you get to me so quickly? I left you back at those apartments," Nado mentioned. Lil Boot replied, "Each time you leave those apartments after picking up, I've trailed behind to ensure your safety. You haven't been alone leaving that place." Nado grinned, placing a hand on his partner's shoulder.

"What are they going to do to you?" asked JT. Nado replied, "Not sure yet. I'll be visiting a lawyer tomorrow to find out."

"It's not too late to come clean, Nado. I can handle it," Lil Boot suggested. Nado glanced at his close friends and stated, "You two mean the world to me, and I'd give my life for either of you. This will just be a minor issue." The following day, Nado met with a lawyer recommended by a friend who reassured him, "Don't worry. I'll keep you informed on the situation."

Nado firmly grasped the lawyer's hand and departed. Three months later, he received a call from his attorney. "Your court date is set for Friday. They're going all-out to bring you down, painting you as a dangerous predator. Don't worry though - we'll fight back," the lawyer reassured Nado. All week, Nado anxiously wondered about the outcome of the upcoming trial.

On Thursday evening, he treated his mother and sister to a lovely dinner at a fancy restaurant, reassuring them everything would be fine in court. While they were savoring their meal, Nado's pager buzzed. Recognizing the number displayed, he excused himself to make a call outside. Lil Boot picked up the call instantly. "Hey, man! We were just talking about you. How are you?"

"I'm good! Mom and Necy are with me; we're about to enjoy dinner together. I'll catch up with you later, and hey, stop worrying," Nado replied confidently. Upon returning to their table, he found Necy already indulging in her dessert. Nado quickly joined her in savoring the sweet treat.

After dinner, Nado headed home with his family and reached out to his friends. "Where are you guys?" JT replied, "We're just cruising around. What's happening on your end?" "Pick me up, and we'll hang out for a bit. I can't stay out too late, though; I need some rest for a big day tomorrow," Nado said.

"Where do you want to go?" asked JT. "How about Club Paradise?" suggested Lil Boot. "Club Paradise it is," agreed Nado. "We'll be there in no time," added Lil Boot. Ending the call, Nado's thoughts drifted back to the earlier conversation with his attorney. He had an influential lawyer, but even that couldn't guarantee leniency from the district attorney during his trial.

Nado faced a difficult choice: accept a plea deal or go to trial. Accepting the plea meant admitting guilt for something he didn't do. However, going to trial put him at a high risk of being wrongly convicted of attempted murder during a robbery. The district attorney was determined to seek the harshest sentence if Nado chose trial. He could turn on his partner for an easier outcome, but that thought never crossed his mind.

Nado faced a crucial decision, one that he had to make alone. After careful consideration, he realized he had no other choice. He kept his conclusion to himself, not even telling his lawyer. He recognized the district attorney's persistence due to Lil Boot causing significant damage to the man. Nado knew this choice would alter his life forever. He had enjoyed the good life, but now it was time to face the consequences. He couldn't share his decision with his partners, especially not with Lil Boot.

Their partnership was built on unity and loyalty – they were all in this together. Knowing Lil Boot wouldn't let Nado take the fall for him made it even more challenging to reveal his intentions. As Nado's partners pulled into the driveway, he greeted them and mentioned that he had some errands to run and would drive. He promised to meet at their usual spot in half an hour while Lil Boot joked about spending his 30 minutes with some attractive young women.

"Fuck you, Lil Boot. See you in half an hour," said Nado. He strolled over to his car, taking a moment to appreciate it before getting in. Knowing he wouldn't be driving it for some time, he felt a twinge of nostalgia. He climbed into the driver's seat, turned the key, and cruised down the road without another word. As Lil Boot completed a U-turn, he pondered Nado's behavior. "He seemed out of it, don't you think?" he commented. JT reassured him, "He's fine. He's just new to all this court stuff." Despite JT's words, Lil Boot couldn't help but worry about his friend as they left the parking lot.

Thirty minutes had passed, and it was time for Nado to meet up with his friends. He pulled into the parking lot only to find it empty. With no sign of Lil Boot or JT, Nado got out of his BMW and set the alarm. Making his way into the club, he was escorted to the VIP area and handed a complimentary bottle of Don Parion champagne.

Nado was about to take his second glass when Lil Boot and JT appeared at the table. Quickly placing his glass down, Nado greeted them both with warm hugs. "Glad you guys could finally make it," Nado teased. "We just got a little caught up," explained Lil Boot with a chuckle. "You know how irresistible we are to some ladies – it's our duty to entertain them!" Nado settled into his seat and watched his friends with amusement in his eyes.

Not long ago, they used to swap shoes to create the illusion of owning many pairs. Now, a single scratch on their $200 sneakers would make them retire the pair. They had faced everything together, and he was sure they'd continue doing so. "This place is wild tonight. If someone can't find a date here, they must be uninterested," said JT. "You're crazy, Don Waun can't compete with me," replied Lil Boot. Nado grinned as he listened to his friends. "Anything catch your eye?" asked Nado.

"I'm just relaxing tonight, spending time with my friends and enjoying life. Memories are priceless," replied Nado. He raised his glass in a toast, downing the remaining drink afterward. They all spent about an hour observing the women in front of their table. Finally, Nado said, "I've had enough for now. You guys have fun and hone your skills. If I didn't have a busy day ahead, I'd stay and show you both a thing or two." Nado got up for what he knew would be their last embrace for quite some time.

Nado exited the club as they watched intently. "Something's off. He mentioned something about time spent. I'm telling you, man, something's not right," said Lil Boot. "Yeah, what's not right is missing that gorgeous woman on my water bed," joked JT. That comment snapped Lil Boot back to the present, pushing his concern to the back of his mind for now.

Waking up with a mild headache, Nado checked the time and realized he had roughly an hour and a half before his court appearance. Deciding to head out early to discuss matters with his lawyer, he stopped by a McDonald's he hadn't visited in over a year. He wanted to greet an old friend who had never left his thoughts.

As Nado was about to enter the fast-food restaurant, he hesitated, recalling Azurie's last words to him during their final meeting. He stared at her face, which seemed even more beautiful than he remembered. Despite Azurie making it clear she didn't want them to cross paths again, Nado couldn't bring himself to go against her wishes. As he turned and walked back towards his car, he unexpectedly found himself gazing into Azurie's enchanting eyes once more.

An urge to dash outside and halt him welled up within her, but the long line of customers held her back. Her typical cheerful smile had faded into a melancholy one as she watched the BMW reverse and exit the parking lot. Over the past year, thoughts of Nado had frequently crossed her mind.

Meanwhile, outside the courtroom, Nado stood frozen, absorbing his attorney's words. The time had come for him to make the most crucial choice of his young life. "Mr. Dexter, have you reached a decision? Whatever your choice, I'm here to support you. However, you must be aware of the potential consequences if we go to trial. The prosecution has two witnesses ready to accuse you in court. While I think I can discredit one of them, dealing with the victim is an entirely different matter. The jury will be presented with images of his injuries and will witness firsthand that he has yet to recover from the assault." Confused, Nado asked, "What are they talking about?"

"Look, we have a tough judge today. I'll talk to the D.A., and perhaps they'll agree to a three-year sentence," proposed his lawyer. Alarmed, Nado replied, "Three years? There is no way I can do that long! You've got to do better than that." His lawyer continued calmly, "Let me finish. I'll request that two of those years be suspended—leaving you with only one mandatory year left to serve, day by day."

"So, what do you think if I can secure that deal for you?" inquired the attorney. Nado pondered over his mother and sister's situation without him. A sudden smile crossed his face as he realized neither he nor his family would be alone, thanks to the unwavering support of his two partners. "If they agree, I'm in." With that, Nado's lawyer left and returned 15 minutes later, ready to face the judge.

As they stood before Judge Slaughter, the judge reviewed the plea bargain with disapproval evident in his shaking head. The courtroom's silence was interrupted by a throat-clearing sound. Nado glanced at his partners' reassuring smiles. Winking at them, he shifted his focus back to the judge, who then spoke up. "It seems both parties have reached an agreement." Judge Slaughter's unwavering gaze fell upon Nado.

"Mr. Dexter, fortune is on your side today. Despite reviewing your clean criminal record and reading the report of your violent actions towards the victim, I must say you're lucky not to be facing a murder charge. You ought to be grateful that the state is showing mercy for your lack of compassion towards another human being. Only because of your clean past am I willing to accept the state's recommendation. Please step forward, Mr. Dexter," declared Judge Slaughter.

Nado, standing bold and calm before Judge Slaughter, received his query of any final words with a respectful "No sir. " The sentencing was given out shortly - "Mr. Dexter, it is hereby ordered by this court that you are sentenced to a term of three years in the State of Alabama's state corrections. It is also ordered by this court that two of those three years be suspended, with one to be served in full. You may take him into custody. This proceeding is adjourned." As this verdict was passed, Nado was taken into custody, concluding the proceedings.

The calm was shattered by Lil Boot's outraged disbelief. "What in the world do you mean to take him into custody?" said Lil Boot. Rising from his seat in shock and anger, he wrestled free from the security officer holding him back. His open hostility towards the judge and the courtroom was rewarded with an order for his immediate arrest for contempt of court. The defiance shone brightly in Lil Boot as the officers moved to subdue him.

Amidst the chaos, Nado tried to defuse the situation. "I accepted it, partner. He didn't give it to me. Listen to me. I need you on the ground to take care of my mom and Necy. Don't do this, and I need you." Said Nado. He looked into Nado's eyes as the security guards approached and cuffed him. This heartfelt plea seemed to calm Lil Boot down momentarily.

In the thick of this tense feud, their friend JT silently watched as both Lil Boot and Nado were led away by security. They walked silently until they reached the holding cell, giving them a chance to further discuss Nado's decision for some time.

"I'm the one who ought to be going, not you," Lil Boot lamented, tears trailing down his cheeks. "We'll step up, my friend," Nado reassured him. "Make sure you and JT look after Mom and Necy." "They won't lack for anything," assured Lil Boot. A mutual understanding passed between them as they shared a hug. Nado whispered into Lil Boot's ear before pulling away, searching his eyes. "Am I my brother's keeper?" Lil Boot's response was immediate and sure. "Yes, you are your brother's keeper." A prison guard interrupted their goodbye to escort Nado to the transport van. Alone for the first time in his life, Nado left behind a courtroom echoing with commotion. Necy provided futile comfort to their distraught mother, sprawled on the floor while JT attempted to lift Mrs. Nell up from her despair. "We'll get through this, Mrs. Nell," he reassured her, "I promise it'll be all right."

A fortnight had passed, and Mrs. Nell started to sense a change in Necy's behavior. No longer was the young girl she knew; Necy had started keeping questionable company, and her nights seemed endless. Inquiries about her brother became infrequent, almost as if he was a forgotten memory. Parallelly, Mrs. Nell noticed a shift in Necy's appearance - could it be exhaustion from her new non-stop lifestyle? One day, while tidying up Necy's room, Mrs. Nell found evidence - a sachet with a substance resembling baking soda. Quietly slipping it into her pocket, she resolved to show it to JT and Lil Boot. If her gut feeling was right, perhaps this mysterious sachet was the missing piece that connected the dots about Necy's sudden transformation.

It was natural to be frightened when you were about to enter life in prison. Nado was no different. He had been stripped naked and sprayed like a dog for bugs. It had been both humbling and humiliating for him, having to bend over and spread his buttock cheeks so that the correction officer could look up his rectum, searching for contraband.

After surviving the receiving area, Nado now stood in the dormitory, looking around. All of a sudden, Nado heard his name shouted from somewhere across the dorm. He looked, and his eyes finally settled on a face that he recognized. It was Shaun from the hood. Everyone watched as Shaun walked to Nado. "Oh man," the guy shouted for everyone to hear. This is the big man on the street. Everything comes through his hands. He supplies quantity and quality of the finest drugs on the streets. I mean, big-time dope boy. My homeboy is a millionaire. He put dat dope out there." While Shaun kept bragging about

Nado, another guy that has been sitting back listening began to ease his way towards Nado.

"Hello, my brothers, my name is Kidar. I couldn't help but overhear your conversation. I don't understand how you can stand here and glorify a man who sells drugs. It takes a weak-minded brother to brag about a man who sells poison to his own black brothers and sisters. It's people like him who have the black race in the position we're in today. "Who the fuck do you think you're talking to? We don't want to hear that Farrakhan ass shit you're talking about. Take that As-salamu alaikum shit to somebody else. We don't want to hear it."

"I only speak the truth to you, my brother. Do you not see a drug problem in your community? Who did you sell your million dollars' worth of drugs to? Surely not Mr. Bo Bo. Look at the destruction that drugs have caused in our communities. Look at all your brother. 80% of these black men here are for selling drugs, robbery, stealing, or dirty urine. All those things have a base factor. Drugs. Sellers get caught and go to prison, and users rob and steal or smoke. Bottomline, the black race is an endangered species. A black man goes into the store and gets caught stealing a size 38 pants when he only wears a size 28 pants. Why? Because he steals for people like you to get the poison you have. A son, father, brother, or uncle is lost, and there's nobody left to guide the next generation. He abandons a kind-hearted woman who then possibly falls prey to corrupt drug dealers like you, and what unfolds next drives me crazy. He leaves a good black woman out there, and one of you dope boys gets her and corrupts her. Now, the little black man gets to see you make your money by selling poison. You don't care because the Lil nigga ain't yours. You just want the mama. If you let them hang around long enough, you put Lil nigga on when he gets 9 or 10. He hangs out on the corner selling your dope at 9 years old. "Here's the scenario: The young boy sees how you earn easy money through illicit means with zero care for him cos he ain't yours: you're just after his mom. If he sticks around long enough with you, then by the time he's 9 or 10 years old, he'd be there standing on the corner peddling your narcotics at such a young age! How often do we see white boys engaging in such illicit activity in their neighborhoods? Exactly - rarely!"

"Naw nigga, you got to stop talking so much. Nado, I'll talk to you after this nigga leave." Nado didn't even see his homeboy leave. He was tuned in on what the guy was now saying. "It's time for the black man to become whole again, and there is only one way for that to happen. We have to take the message to the lost brothers and sisters. We have to take our neighborhoods and kids back from the dealers, my brothers. I know you don't understand, or should I say, you can't relate to what I'm saying right now, but I would like to invite you to join us at service tonight. Brother Faheem will be speaking tonight. I think you would enjoy him. Tell you what, I'll walk back through before service and check on you. As-Salaam Alaikum."

CHAPTER FIVE

Consequences and Reflections: Nado's New Path

The man turned away and strolled off, leaving Nado deep in thought. As Nado headed to his bunk, he spotted his friend approaching. "You're not considering attending that prejudiced gathering, right? They only want to brainwash you with their 'white man is the devil' nonsense." Shaun stopped mid-sentence, noticing Nado's distracted demeanor. "Hey, I'll catch up with you later. My buddies just got our stash, and we're about to light up." Shaun walked off as memories overwhelmed Nado. Before being drawn into this lifestyle, he had despised drugs for shattering his family. Yet, he had done the very thing he hated. He could now envision people he once admired rummaging through trash for food. He realized that he had inflicted the same pain on others as he had suffered – taking a father away. Intrigued, he decided to attend the evening's service.

As Nado sat in the dorm, thoughts of Azurie filled his mind, wondering if she ever thought of him. Thirty minutes until the service began. Kidar, having already dressed, was now wandering in search of Nado. Despite checking each dorm room twice, he was unable to locate him. Disappointed, he headed towards the service, where he unexpectedly saw Nado's face. As-Salaam-alaikum - "I'm Kidar; I apologize for not introducing myself earlier." Nado replied with his name, and they shook hands before sitting together as the service started. With keen interest, Nado listened to the introduction of the speaker. "It is my honor to introduce to you our leader, Faheem," Nado observed as a short young man approached the man who introduced Minister Faheem. They shook hands, exchanged greetings, and saluted each other. "As-Salaam-Alaikum, my brother," said Faheem. "WA-Alaikum-Salaam," the crowd replied.

"In the name of Allah, the most gracious and merciful, to whom all praises are due, I greet you. How do we perceive the devil? The Holy Bible describes him as one of the most beautiful angels from heaven. Yet, we often imagine an entity with horns and a pointed tail. If I were seeking understanding about the devil, how should I envisage him? Whose perception is correct—man's or the Bible's? What if I tell you that the devil is a spirit capable of inhabiting anyone? The devil surrounds us, Black Man. Black people in America suffer under falsehoods while truth echoes in their ears. They witness evidence of truth but reject it.

Those are the words of the Honorable Elijah Muhammad. What do Muslims believe? We believe that we, the black race, are God's chosen people—those rejected and despised. If slave masters genuinely cared for so-called Negroes, why start any relationship with deception? This is because their souls harbor deceitful spirits. Anticipating an end to slavery, slave masters devised a hollow plan: The Emancipation Proclamation—promising freed slaves 40 acres and a mule—but never fulfilled it.

As Muslims, we believe it's time for self-determination—an opportunity for descendants of slaves to establish their own separate state or territory within America.

We also believe that our former slave masters are obligated to provide fertile and mineral-rich land. Over years of evident struggle, we have realized that coexisting with them in peace and equality is impossible despite providing them with 400 years of our labor and blood. In return, we received some of the most inhumane treatments in history. Our contributions and the suffering imposed upon us by white America justify our demand for complete separation in a state or territory of our own. We desire that every black man or woman has the freedom to accept or reject separation from slave masters who exploit our beautiful black sisters in plantation houses so he can put his evil hands on her and have his way with her.

Minister Faheem looked up and acknowledged Nado. "I see that we have a new brother with us tonight. All praise be to Allah. Thank you for coming, and I hope you will hear something inspiring in your pursuit of truth." Minister Faheem turned back to the audience. "People perceive us as a racist group, equating us with the Klan, Skin Heads, and Southern Brotherhood. They claim the only difference between us and them except for the fact that we are black. If they label us as racists, they must also address the racism among their own brothers because there are white Muslims all over the world.

I have yet to see a black Klansman or a black man join the Southern Brotherhood. So, how can they label us as racists? We invite everyone to become Muslims and follow the teachings of the Honorable Elijah Muhammad. We only teach, hoping that black men and women will stand up and represent themselves with pride and dignity. We want them to return to their original positions as rulers of the universe. It's difficult right now, with black-on-black crime and drug sales destroying brilliant minds.

The black community built the world, only to have it taken by others. The cleansing starts with us. Black People must stand strong and reclaim their neighborhoods. We can't wait for others to help – those who seek to keep drugs in our communities, knowing they'll cause chaos. They lied from the beginning, and their descendants will lie until the end. Stand up, black community, and be recognized as a force to be reckoned with.

Nado returned to the dorm, holding various literature pieces. His thoughts weren't on the texts, though; they were focused on something the minister said during service. When acknowledging Nado, he had used a word Nado couldn't forget - "ambitious." His thoughts drifted to Azurie; during their dinner date, she had told him their ambitions differed. Now he understood what she meant.

Nado regretted not getting to know Azurie better, but he promised himself that he would see her again. This time, he wanted to be prepared. To do so, he needed to become knowledgeable about her beliefs. Nado spent his days studying Muslim literature and his nights attending services. He was determined to learn everything he could about the religion.

He discovered that F.O.I. stood for "Fruit of Islam," referring to the military training of Muslim men in North America. He learned that military training involved tactics, maneuvers, and establishing a foothold in enemy territory. Furthermore, it implied war. Nado also found out that Allah was the Muslim name for God and that Muslims read from a book called the Quran, unlike the Holy Bible.

Nado realized that the F.O.I. was an army like no other, with members few in number but possessing a superior mission. They believed that Allah and their messenger, the honorable Elijah

Muhammad, made them more powerful than their enemies. Nado read about what Muslims called the original man—an idea that originated in Africa. This original man was brought to the United States through trickery and deception before being sold into slavery and forced to abandon his original name for his white slave master's surname.

Nado recalled the movie Roots, which depicted hooded white men hanging Black people and bringing Kunta Kinte to America. Kunta Kinte was beaten until he reluctantly accepted the name Toby. Nado finally understood the reasoning behind this act: it was a means of control and submission.

Nado was eager to explore the differences between the perspectives of the original man and the white man while maintaining an open mind. He understood that uncovering the truth required considering all possibilities. Whenever he encountered something perplexing, he sought answers. He learned that Black people were once not allowed to read, and their knowledge stemmed from what was taught or read to them by white slave masters. This uneducated and degraded state was passed down through generations. Occasionally, a rebellious Black man would resist, prompting the slave master to either kill him or force another enslaved person to beat him into submission in front of the others, instilling fear. Reflecting on his own life and privileges, Nado decided it was time for him to take a stand.

At the next gathering, Nado joined the Nation of Islam and became a dedicated follower of the teachings of the Honorable Elijah Muhammad. Within six months, his knowledge surpassed that of many other members. On the eve of his sixth month, Nado approached Assistant Coordinator Shabazz to express his desire to become a minister and consider changing his name. Shabazz wasn't surprised, as Nado's thirst for knowledge had been evident. He relayed Nado's request to Head Coordinator Minister Faheem, who placed Nado in ministry training classes taught by himself.

In a short time, Nado rose from lieutenant to captain. At his last meeting before returning home, he gathered with his new family one final time. Minister Faheem said, "You rose through the ranks quickly due to your willingness and desire to learn. Though you've reached captain here, you must repeat this course upon your return to freedom. To become a minister, you'll need to go to Chicago and meet a national representative of the Honorable Elijah Muhammad for ordination. I see great potential in you as a strong soldier for our cause. Regarding your name change, that can be done more quickly once you leave here. Do you have any parting words for the brothers?"

Nado stood and addressed his comrades, saying, "As-Salaam-Alaikum. I arrived here a year ago with only one goal - completing 365 days and going home. I never intended to meet anyone or make new friends. However, I am grateful, all praise to Allah, for the chance to listen and grasp the knowledge I have acquired during my stay. Armed with this knowledge, I will strive to improve myself and my people by continuing to learn and teach what I have learned to my black brothers and sisters. I will encourage them to stand up and reclaim the pride of the original man. We have a plague; my brothers and I used to be a significant part of that plague. Today, I make this promise: you will hear of me and my works."

Nado stepped forward and gave his final greeting to Minister Faheem. Unable to fall asleep that night, he tossed and turned in anticipation of the morning sun. Eventually, he drifted off, only to be awakened by an officer who informed him that his family had arrived to pick him up.

As Nado walked down the hall towards the front gate, he observed an unusually large crowd for that time of the morning. Hearing the words As-Salaam-Alaikum, he realized the entire Nation of Islam community had gathered to bid him farewell. He greeted each of them and stopped before Kidar.

"I will never forget you and the world you introduced me to," Nado said. "Had you not taken the time that day, I would still be blind. You have my address; use it. Let me know how you're doing." After embracing Kidar for a few seconds, Nado turned and walked through the gates into the arms of his tearful mother as JT Dollar and Lil Boot stood back, watching the emotional reunion.

"Where is Necy, Mama?" Nado asked. Mrs. Nell replied, "She wasn't home when we left. How are you feeling, dear?" Nado responded, "I just need to get away from this place." They all smiled as he turned to his friends, who hadn't changed a bit since he left. Both were well-dressed and adorned with gold chains and rings. He said, "It seems life has been treating my brothers well."

They hugged and walked towards the car. JT said, "The world awaits, my friend. Everything is still going according to plan – we've even been discussing expansion." Lil Boot smiled at Nado but didn't receive one in return. Nado replied, "Let's focus on getting home so I can spend time with Mom and Necy."

He put his arm around his mother's shoulder and asked about dinner plans before sitting next to her in the back seat. From that moment on, he tried to leave the past behind – but knew there was still unfinished business to attend to.

Mrs. Nell asked about his time away, curious whether it was like what they show on TV. Nado turned and smiled, admitting it wasn't as extreme as portrayed but definitely not a place anyone would want to be. Just a small taste was enough for a lifetime.

As they arrived at the house, Nado admired the familiar exterior – unchanged from the day he left. His mother praised Lil Boot and JT for their help in maintaining it while they smiled back graciously.

"You can count on them," said Nado as he patted both of them on the shoulders before asking if their contact details were unchanged. They nodded in affirmation, and he promised to call them after settling back in at home.

As they entered the house together, Mrs. Nell finally felt relief knowing her son had returned safely. She listened as Nado expressed his desire for a hot bath – something he had been dreaming about since his departure, as showers were all that were available in the institution, he had been in.

With thoughts of a peaceful bath, he ventured towards the bathroom but made a quick detour to greet his little sister Necy. He remembered his mother's earlier statement about Necy's absence and sensed that something wasn't quite right. With a deep breath, he reached for her door handle, anticipating the warm embrace from his sister.

"What's going on, Boss Player?" Lil Boot asked over the phone. "What's your plan for today?" Boss Player replied, "Just holding it together, bro. I got this girl I met recently, and I need to talk to you about something. When can we meet up?" Lil Boot knew Boss Player wanted some drugs to share with his girl, so he asked where they should meet.

Boss Player suggested Lil Boot meet his girl someday because she was stunning. They agreed to meet at the Club House in 30 minutes. This would give Boss Player time to drop off his girl before meeting Lil Boot.

Boss Player had met his girl, Necy, at a club earlier, and despite her claiming to be 21, he knew she wasn't telling the truth. Her age didn't bother him since he was all about having a good time. He had heard rumors about her brother being a big-time drug dealer and being sent to prison but didn't care much about it.

Boss Player told Necy he would drop her off at his house while taking care of business and advised her not to touch his phone while he was gone. Necy kept quiet, reflecting on her previous partners since her brother went to prison.

Her first partner, Kane, spent all his money on cocaine, which Necy wouldn't touch. She left him due to his inability to provide for her lifestyle. Peanut followed – older, successful, and also into cocaine. He could provide for her and eventually convinced her to try it herself.

However, Peanut grew bored of Necy and moved on to someone else, which left Necy searching for another friend— one who shared a love for snorting cocaine. Enter Pretty Tony in the picture—a wild party guy who preferred crack cocaine but rarely had the powder that Necy desired.

One day, when she was desperate for a high, Necy tried crack for the first time using Pretty Tony's pipe. The experience was unforgettable, and unlike any high she'd felt before. Amidst a haze of daily powder snorting, she'd settle into the room with Pretty Tony, losing hours to smoking rocks while he was away. Necy found herself irresistibly drawn to the secret corners where Pretty Tony stashed his goods. Alone and wide-eyed, she'd often be waiting bug-eyed when he returned home.

But one fateful day, Pretty Tony stormed home to discover his stash had completely vanished. Fuming with frustration, he confronted Necy, his voice a mix of anger and urgency, demanding, "Where the hell is my stuff, Necy?" Ignoring him, she remained fixated on the outside world through the curtain's gap, as if engrossed in an unseen drama.

Fed up and fueled by a mix of irritation and disbelief, Pretty Tony seized Necy from behind, pulling her away from the window. "Tell me, Necy! Where's my damn stash?" he bellowed. Breaking her detached silence, she coolly replied, "They're out there, Tony. Didn't you notice them when you walked in? I flushed it all so they couldn't lay their hands on it."

Tony, unaffected by whatever substances Necy had ingested, remained composed. He'd put up with a lot, but this crossed a line. He spat out with seething determination, "You've pushed it too far this time, bitch. You're out of here. I want you gone right now." That night, Necy walked out the door, wandering aimlessly on the streets until she stumbled upon a refuge: a nightclub, the very same place where she'd first met Boss Player.

As she readied herself to step out of the car, she shared a bittersweet smile with Boss Player, communicating a mixture of melancholy and anticipation.

Without a single word, Necy shut the car door and made her way to Boss Player's apartment entrance. Suddenly, a thought struck her - today was the day her brother would be released from prison. She pondered whether he would notice the changes in her. Just the other day, while gazing into the mirror, she noticed her face seemingly dwindling. The reflection staring back at her felt like that of a stranger with vacant eyes. Chalking it up to exhaustion, she dismissed the notion, although her appetite had also waned. Despite her love for good food, she'd been settling for fast food and quick bites like candy bars and chips.

Stepping inside, Necy headed to the phone and dialed a number. The automated voice chimed, "You have reached the Dexter residence. Leave a brief message at the tone, and we will return your call." Hanging up, she sank onto the couch. The house seemed enveloped in an eerie stillness. Necy remained seated, awaiting Boss Player's return.

Nado softly pushed the door open, only to find Necy's room empty. Where could she be at this hour? It was clear she wasn't home. Perhaps she'd ventured out in search of a job. Pushing aside his concerns about Necy, he focused on his immediate need – a relaxing soak in a warm bath.

CHAPTER SIX

Crossroads of Change: Nado's Awakening

Quietly re-entering his own room, Nado observed his surroundings, unchanged since he last left them. Heading to the dresser, he retrieved fresh underclothes and headed to the bathroom. As Nado prepared to turn on the faucet, his gaze fell on a bottle of bubble bath perched on the tub's edge. With a self-assured smile, he decided, "Why not?" After filling the tub about three-quarters full, he turned off the water, undressed, and slipped into the inviting warmth. Resting his head at the edge of the tub, Nado let his eyes drift shut, descending into a contemplative trance.

Lil Boot watched as Boss Player's car pulled into the Waffle House parking lot, aptly nicknamed Club House. A spot where everyone gathered after hitting the club scene. Lil Boot was cautious about phone conversations; he suspected the Feds or the Jump Out Boys might be listening. Trusting Boss Player wasn't easy. Rumor had it that Boss Player's former partner, once a big player, now languished in federal prison. It was all hearsay, but two partners down were concerned. Lil Boot had reason to be wary.

He observed Boss Player stepping out of the car and heading toward him. Boss Player's voice boomed out with a shout, "What's up, Lil Boo!" The last part was cut off by his excitement. He sternly looked into Boss Player's eyes as if saying, "We're not on friendly terms right now." Boss Player picked up on the vibe but still felt a surge of irritation.

"Wait a sec, Lil..." Boss Player began, but Lil Boot's interruption fueled his anger. "Don't ever treat me like a kid again. I don't care what you've heard, but I don't mess around. You think you can play me like a fool?" Lil Boot fired back, "What makes you think I've heard anything? You should know the rules of the game. Are you here to chat or to get down to business?"

Boss Player's fists clenched, but he restrained himself. He had a mission and a honey to get back to. Lil Boot offered a snarky remark, "Nice shirt. How much did it cost?" Boss Player replied, "It's not that pricey. Paid a hundred bucks for it. It has to be nice for the player."

The scene unfolded with an air of mystery, where actions spoke louder than words. Lil Boot's movements were as deliberate as a chess player's, pulling a hundred-dollar package from a concealed spot between his legs. He placed it discreetly beside Boss Player, avoiding even a glance in his direction. The fear of being caught on camera while handling his illicit dealings haunted him, leading him to move like a shadow and keep conversations to a hushed minimum.

A casual observer would mistake Lil Boot for a mere listener, seemingly engrossed in the chatter of the other person. Once the exchange was made, Boss Player left without uttering a word, Lil Boot's earlier implication still echoing in his mind.

A few moments later, the tension thickened when Lil Boot's voice broke through the quiet air, asking JT Dollar a thought-provoking question about Necy's drug habit. "What do you think, JT?" asked Lil Boot, referring to Necy's drug habit. "Should we tell Nado?" As they drove away, JT pondered how to respond. He couldn't break the news about the cocaine Mrs. Nell found in Necy's room without sugarcoating it. Knowing he had to act soon due to the devastating effects of cocaine on users with no means to support their addiction, JT recalled confronting Necy after discovering the small package. She denied ownership, blaming Nado instead. Her weight loss was another red flag.

Recollections of a recent encounter with Boss Player resurfaced in Lil Boot's mind. The phrase "the little bitch is down for anything" played on a loop, triggering his curiosity. The type of "honey" who would be willing to do anything seemed unmistakably tied to the world of addiction, where control was ceded to the power of substances.

Lil Boot's thoughts crystallized, leading him to a bold conclusion. He suspected a connection between the mysterious "little honey" and Necy. "Do you think Boss Player was referring to Necy?" JT's affirmation firmed up the possibility. "That's the million-dollar question." Their actions were driven by the desire to uncover the truth and potentially rescue Necy from her downward spiral.

The gravity of the situation hung in the air as Lil Boot contemplated revealing Necy's struggles to Nado. "It's crucial we tell Nado," said JT, looking at Lil Boot. "If anyone can help her open up, it's him." Hoping she wasn't too far gone, they wondered how Nado would react given his father's history. The discussion shifted to finding out who supplied Necy and a recent conversation about a woman being "down for anything." This description reminded them of drug-addicted women who'd lost control over their decision-making.

Their car maneuvered through the surroundings, carrying not just the physical weight of their presence but also the weight of their choices. "I think I know where to start looking," muttered Lil Boot. "Do you think Boss Player meant Necy?" The hunt for answers began, as they decided to start by investigating Boss Player's dwelling. They considered revisiting Boss Player and pretending they'd changed their minds about partying to get a glimpse of this mysterious woman.

With Necy's well-being on their minds, the two shared a moment of introspection, acknowledging that Nado's intervention might be the lifeline Necy needed. The uncertainty of Necy's state hung heavily, and all they could do was hope that she hadn't spiraled too far down the rabbit hole.

In the midst of their conversation, Lil Boot's musings took an unexpected turn. The drug trade's web of consequences was entwined with the lives of countless people, including the vulnerable. The realization dawned on Lil Boot that the repercussions of this particular drug deal would be profound. The anticipation of retribution was palpable as he pondered the fate of whoever was responsible.

Meanwhile, Nado's quiet moments of meditation were interrupted by a knock on the bathroom door. The familiar voice of his mother broke his trance, grounding him in reality. His daydreams gave way to his surroundings, realizing he had been soaking for far too long. He reassured her and asked if Necy had returned home. After a pause, she informed him that Necy still hadn't arrived. Nado then focused on finishing his bath and enjoying his first day of freedom with his family, blissfully unaware of the challenges they all faced.

Necy's nerves were on edge as she watched Boss Player's car pull into the driveway. Anticipation and anxiety churned within her, manifesting in the way she nervously chewed her fingernails. A sudden bout of unease struck her, a familiar sensation that always seemed to precede her drug use. It was as if her body anticipated the hit before her mind even acknowledged it.

With urgency, she leaped from her spot and sprinted down the hall to the bathroom. Just as she shut the bathroom door behind her, Boss Player entered the house. His voice, smooth yet authoritative, echoed through the silence as he called out for his "Little Honey." "Big Boss is home, and I've got something for you," he said. However, her response was nothing but silence.

Strolling through the house, Boss Player suddenly sensed where his Little Honey was hiding. He could smell the scent. The faint aroma guided him to the bathroom door. He knocked lightly and posed a somewhat absurd question, pretending to brew coffee. He found himself asking a ridiculous question, "What are you doing in there? I'm making you a pot of coffee. Can't you smell it brewing?"

Necy knew her response was equally silly, but sometimes playful banter called for exchanging absurd remarks. She chuckled and admitted, "Okay, you got me."

The urgency in Boss Player's tone resonated as he instructed her to hurry up. He left a small package for her on the kitchen counter, then made his way to the front door. But before he could open it, the doorbell rang, interrupting his plans. With an inward sigh, he peered through the peephole, only to find Tina, another one of his "Little Honeys," on the other side.

Fuck, he thought as he looked at the face of Tina. Regaining his composure, he swung the door open. "What's going on, love?" he asked, extending his arms for a warm embrace. However,

Tina disregarded the affectionate gesture and strode past him into the house.

"I need some money." Tina frowned and looked at Boss Player. "What is that goddamn smell?" She asked. She didn't give Boss Player time to answer her question before she continued talking. "I don't have all day; I got an appointment to get my hair done, and I've got to go the mall and get this outfit before someone else gets it. Are you gonna give me some money or what?"

Necy, hearing Tina's voice, cracked the bathroom door slightly, her curiosity piqued but her wariness keeping her hidden. She didn't recognize Tina and decided it was best to stay out of sight.

Boss Player, aware of Necy's presence, needed to manage the situation carefully. He led Tina outside, his focus on preventing a confrontation between the two women. He wasn't worried about Necy, and his concerns came from Tina. She was a fighter, and he knew that if Tina saw Necy, she would try to fight on the spot.

After guiding Tina outside, Boss strode towards the car, simultaneously reaching for the door handle and gently holding her arm. As he opened the driver's side door and climbed into the front seat, Tina remained standing, her gaze fixed on him. Boss Player fumbled with the glove compartment while a grin spread across Tina's face as she noticed two attractive guys cruising by slowly.

"I guess you don't get the million-dollar. Damn, she sure is fine." Said JT Dollar. Lil Boot responded, "In a way, I wanted it to be Necy, so I would have a reason to bust that snitching son of bitch's head.

Meanwhile, Nado's daydreams turned real as he unveiled his prized possession, his BMW, hidden under a tarp in the garage. The prospect of driving it, once a mere fantasy, was now tangible. Sliding into the driver's seat, his hand gripping the steering wheel, he brought the car to life with a turn of the key. The roar of the engine confirmed the fulfillment of his aspirations.

Mrs. Nell sat alone in her room, the weight of her thoughts overshadowing the happiness of her son's return. The day had begun on a high note, with Nado's long-awaited homecoming filling her with joy. Yet, the reality of life's challenges had crept back in, reminding her of a difficult conversation she couldn't avoid any longer.

With a heavy heart, she made the decision to cancel their plans for a celebratory dinner. Instead, she opted to stay home and address the elephant in the room with Nado – his sister's situation. As she sat there, she absentmindedly looked down at her intertwined fingers resting between her knees.

Meanwhile, Necy had just finished smoking the package Boss Player had given her. Sitting near the window, she glanced outside periodically, her mind seemingly distant from the words Boss Player was speaking. He tried to engage her, his impatience growing. "Come to the bedroom, my sweet honey," he urged, driven by both desire and a belief that Necy owed him.

However, Necy's mind was elsewhere, lost in the haze of whatever she had just smoked. Her fingers fiddled restlessly as she peered through the curtains, seemingly detached from the present moment. Boss Player's attempts to regain her attention fell on deaf ears.

Meanwhile, in a different setting, Lil Boot and JT found themselves driving in silence. JT's fingers danced over his phone as he scrolled through his contacts, his focus eventually landing on a particular number. Curiosity piqued, Lil Boot questioned, "Whose number are you looking up, JT?"

Looking up from his phone, JT explained, "I'm calling Nado to catch up and let him know what's happening. It's better he hears it from us than from someone else." Aware that Nado's mood was currently upbeat, they understood the importance of timing.

As the phone rang in his ear, JT prepared to hang up if no one answered. Suddenly, the ringing ceased, and a voice broke the silence. "Hello, may I help you?" JT's response followed, "Hello, Mrs. Nell, How are you doing?" The concern in his tone was palpable.

In a somber tone, Mrs. Nell replied, "Hello, JT, I'm not doing too well right now." JT, alarmed, inquired if she was sick. She clarified, "No, not physically. I need to talk to Nado about his sister, but I'm torn. His spirits are high, and I don't want to dampen his mood after all he's been through."

Curious about Nado's whereabouts, JT asked, "Where is he?" Mrs. Nell shared, "He's in his room getting dressed. Why do you ask?" JT assured her, "Don't worry, Mrs. Nell. Lil Boot and I were thinking the same thing. He needs to know, and he has to be told."

An unspoken understanding lingered in the silence that followed. While everyone recognized the necessity of informing Nado, the question remained: Who would bear the responsibility? As the weight of the situation pressed on, Mrs. Nell posed the question, "So, what's your plan?"

JT responded with resolve, "We're on our way to your place. It's time to do what needs to be done." Another brief silence hung in the air before Mrs. Nell agreed, "Alright, I'll do my part and stall him. I'll be waiting for you." The call ended just as a knock echoed through her room. She rose to answer, asking, "Who is it?"

"What are you up to in there, Mama? Aren't you ready to hit the town and paint it red with your son?" Nado's voice was full of excitement. If emotions could be mixed into a cocktail, Mrs. Nell was sipping from that glass. She replied, "Just give me a few more minutes, baby. I'll be all set." The faint sound of Nado's footsteps retreated as he left the doorway. What she had to do would certainly spoil Nado's homecoming, but it was something that had to be done.

Frustrated and disgusted, Boss Player walked up to Necy and pulled her away from the window. "I don't have time for this kind of nonsense." Necy resisted his grasp, desperately yearning to return to the window where the police were cautiously navigating around the house. That was the last straw. The Boss wasn't about to tolerate this behavior.

"Let me take you home, honey. "You might need some rest," said Boss Player. Necy managed to break free from Boss's grasp and returned to the window. The cops were gone, vanished into thin air. Boss could only shake his head as he looked at Necy staring out of the window.

He pivoted, keys in hand, striding over to the counter before making his way to the curtain-bound Necy. He gripped her by the elbow, and hesitantly, Necy allowed Boss to pull her away from the window and lead her through the door.

Meanwhile, Nado stood before the mirror, taking in the impeccable fit of his Kenneth Cole suit, untouched for a whole year. His self-admiration was interrupted by the doorbell's chime. Casting a final approving glance at his reflection, he headed for the door. Without bothering to inquire about the visitor, he swung it open. His two best friends were on the other side.

"What's up? We were just riding around and decided to drop in on our friend," said JT Dollar. Nado's response was swift, "Bad timing, my brothers. I'm about to take Mom out for dinner." Nado looked at his friends, expecting them to say they'd catch up with him later, but they just stood there with somber looks on their faces. Their expressions gave Nado that gut feeling that something wasn't right, and his first thought went to Necy.

As the doorbell rang, Mrs. Nell finished getting ready and made her way to the living room. She entered just in time to catch Nado's inquiry to Lil Boot and JT about what was wrong. Breaking in with her warm smile, she asked, "What brings you two over?"

Nado sensed something was off about her smile—it lacked its usual authenticity. Nado called for a timeout and voiced his confusion. "Hold on a moment. You guys dropped us off with the plan that Mom and I were going out. I said I'd hit you up once we're back. But here you are before we've even left. Can someone please explain what's going on? Is it about Necy?"

Lil Boot and JT glanced at Mrs. Nell, who seemed weighed down as she gazed at the floor. Nado urged, "Someone start talking."

Mrs. Nell said, "Let's go to the kitchen and sit down so I can get everyone something to drink. We can talk in there." Once everyone was seated with their drinks, Mrs. Nell began. "Nado, I don't want you to speak until we're done explaining what's happening. It started when I was cleaning Necy's room and found a small bag of white substance that resembled baking soda. I showed it to Lil Boot and JT, who told me what it was. Necy has been staying out all night and not eating, and her appearance has worsened. That's why she wasn't with us when we picked you up. I believe your sister is using drugs, Nado."

Everyone expected an explosion of anger from Nado, but it never came. Instead, he sat there, lost in thought. When he finally spoke, it was hard to believe this was the same person who left a year ago.

Nado began, "Listen, I guess now is a good time to reveal the real me." He turned to his friends. Before I went away, our life seemed good, right? We set out with goals, and we surpassed them by leaps and bounds. We've fueled addiction in countless Black men and women and turned many people into drug addicts. But that chapter is over, Lil Boot. It's over, JT. I never truly grasped the harm we inflicted on our own community. And now, that poison is in my own home. Now, I've found a new path—Islam. You two are my closest friends in this world. Just as I once brought you into the game, now I ask you to leave it with me. Today, I declare that drugs and those who sell them are my enemies. I've never led you astray before, and I won't now. You're either with me or against me. Understand this—I will become an undeniable force. I don't need your answer now. What I do need is to find Necy. Find out who's responsible, no matter how." Turning to his mother, Nado concluded with a solemn "Allah is good."

As Boss Player turned onto Necy's street, a jolt of surprise shot through him – there sat Lil Boot's car in her driveway. "What the hell is that guy's car doing here?" Boss Player muttered under his breath. Necy seemed lost in her own world as if he hadn't said a word. The intensity of the situation had taken its toll on her. "I'll address this shit once she's back in her right mind," Boss Player whispered. He pulled up beside the curb and waited for Necy to exit the car, but she remained motionless, fixated on some distant thought. Frustrated, he reached across and opened the car door. With a childlike obedience, Necy stepped out.

In a swift motion, Boss Player closed the door and drove off without a word. Inside the house, Nado's ears caught the sound of a car door shutting. He cautiously approached the living room and peeked through the peephole. No car was in sight, but what he did see almost brought tears to his eyes. The sister he had left behind a year ago was not the same person he now saw, moving like a zombie towards the front door.

Before Necy could even reach for the doorknob, Nado swung the door open. Gazing at her with pained eyes brimming with tears, he struggled to hold back his emotions. Finally, Necy raised her head, locking eyes with Nado. At that moment, the fog seemed to lift, and tears streamed down her face. Nado stepped onto the porch, enfolding his sister in a warm embrace. Together, they stood, tears mingling, finding solace in each other's arms.

As the minutes passed and Nado didn't return to the kitchen, everyone rose from their seats and moved toward the living room. The sight of Nado and Necy standing on the porch, locked in a tearful embrace, touched Mrs. Nell's heart. She joined them, wrapping her arms around the two most precious souls in her life.

"I'm home now, and I promise things will be okay," Nado whispered. Take her inside, give her a bath, and make sure she doesn't leave the house. You two, come with me. Nado stopped by the shed where he had hidden his money and grabbed a stack of bills. He and his partners first visited the printing company and had 2,000 flyers printed, advertising a free barbecue for the entire community and the surrounding area. JT and Lil Boot were hosting this barbecue as a welcome home party for Nado. With JT and Lil Boot leading the charge, the event was bound to draw attention. If someone had forgotten about Nado since he'd been away, his partners were certainly well-known, and who in their right mind could refuse an invitation to an all-you-can-eat free barbecue?

Next, they hit the radio station. Nado parted with some cash to ensure the barbecue announcement blared every half hour right from the moment he slipped the money into the manager's palm. Flyers were dispatched to malls, strategically tucked onto car windshields, and affixed to poles by hired hands. Nado aimed for prime visibility – anywhere eyes could catch a glimpse. As the day unfolded, the town buzzed with talk of the upcoming picnic.

Nado, JT, and Lil Boot embarked on a mission, storming each housing project, knocking on doors, and personally extending an invitation to the free shindig. The gears were grinding, and the plan was underway. Nado was confident people would show up; he had his role laid out. That wasn't the issue gnawing at him.

His concern was JT and Lil Boot. Could they break free from the grip of the life they had become accustomed to? The answer would arrive in a week's time. "You got a purpose behind all this, Nado," JT voiced his curiosity. "I mean, sure, close friends and family could throw a nice homecoming bash. But what's really driving you, man?" Nado pondered, taking a moment before responding.

"Have you ever considered how many good people struggle in life due to drug addiction?" Nado asked. "They live day by day, barely surviving. I want to give back to some of these individuals who have contributed to our lives. You can understand my perspective, right?"

No words came from Lil Boot or JT. The streets played cold, and if it had its hooks in you, tough luck. "Can you fathom the cost?" JT asked skeptically. "I mean, every Tom, Dick, and Harry will roll up for free food. You're looking at dropping twenty grand, maybe more. Chicken, beef, charcoal, buns, music, drinks – it piles up, man. Do you get it?" JT pressed.

"But JT, there's a bigger prize down the line, trust me," Nado assured him. "There is a bigger pot of gold. Check this out, and I need to go over to the phone booth and look up a number. I'll be right back." Said Nado. As Nado walked away, JT leaned into Lil Boot. "Yo, my dawg, what's the fuck do you think is going on with Nado? Can a year away from society twist someone's mind so much that he starts giving everything away? Something's up."

Lil Boot offered his perspective. "It runs deeper, JT. Whatever Nado's got cooking, it's got to be a major purpose behind it. And it's our duty to back him, whatever the deal is." JT shook his head, concern etched on his face. "What about the game, Boot? The style, the rides, the ladies – Nado wants us to give up all that shit? He's my dawg, but damn, man. I ain't punching a clock for no goddam white dude. Not JT Dollar."

"I hear you, my dawg. I get where you're coming from. Let's just roll with it and see how things play out." Lil Boot's mind wandered back exactly one year from today. A whole year had been swapped for something he had done, a sacrifice that etched an unbreakable bond between him and Nado. There wasn't a force on this planet that could make him hesitate when Nado needed a favor.

The echo of Nado's whispered words still resonated in Lil Boot's ear, just as they had when he was about to be taken away into custody. That memory brought a grin to his face. Yes, he had taken up the role of being his brother's keeper, a commitment that was now inked in eternity.

Nado sauntered over to his two closest buddies, spotting Lil Boot's grin. "What's got you grinning, my dawg?" he quizzed. Lil Boot shot back, "Just reminiscing about some words that stuck with me."

Lil Boot piped up, "So, what's the plan now?" Lil Boot inquired, to which Nado swiftly replied, "I've got a quick errand to run, fellas. I'll catch you on the flip side for a night of fun. Meanwhile, do some digging and find out who's been rolling with Necy." With that, Nado turned on his heels and started to walk off.

"I guess where he's going, he doesn't need a ride," JT remarks. Without further ado, Lil Boot and JT strolled over to the car, hopped in, and drove away, leaving the mysteries of the day to unfold.

Necy had taken a bath and was now sitting in her room, contemplating the pain she saw in Nado's eyes. Her mother had lovingly bathed her, just as she had done when Necy was a child. Despite feeling the love from her mother and brother, something deep inside stopped her from accepting it. Instead, that inner voice urged her to sneak out of the house through the window.

Her mother had strategically positioned herself in a chair in the living room, allowing her to see down the hall where Necy's room was located. She wasn't taking any chances of Necy leaving through the back door while she sat watching television, waiting for Nado to come home.

All was quiet in the Dexter household. Mrs. Nell's baby girl was getting some much-needed rest, and soon, her son would be home to help. Everything was peaceful at their residence. Unbeknownst to Mrs. Nell, the faint squeak of the window went unnoticed as Necy carefully slid it up.

Nado walked a few blocks to his destination, aware that he was taking a risk yet convinced it was worth it. He composed himself before entering the building, where, as expected, he was searched for weapons. Once cleared, Nado took a seat and listened intently to the words being spoken.

A man Nado had seen before was speaking, but they had never met. As the talk neared its end, the speaker invited any guests to stand and introduce themselves. Once again, Nado found himself in the spotlight, being the only guest in the audience. He stood and spoke with authority.

"As-Salaam-Alaikum. First, I'd like to express my gratitude to Allah, the most gracious and merciful, to whom all praises are due. With your permission, I'd like to share a brief reflection." The speaker nodded, and Nado continued. "A few years ago, I made a regrettable choice without considering its impact on others. I purchased jewelry, televisions, and other items that I knew were likely stolen from those who needed them more than me. During my journey, I met someone but lost them before truly getting to know them. Yet, they remained in my thoughts. Eventually, I went to prison, where I was introduced to Islam.

That was the moment I realized why I had lost this person. I can still recall their question and the subsequent statement on that day. They inquired about my workplace, and when I didn't reply immediately, they said, "I don't think we'll be seeing each other again, as our ambitions differ." Back then, I failed to grasp the meaning of "different ambitions," but my study of Islam has since shed light on it. The lifestyle I led contradicted everything this person believed in.

While they focused on empowering our people, I was unintentionally harming them with my drugs. Today, I came here with two purposes. First, I want to join you all in seeking knowledge and allowing Allah to guide me through the everyday struggles we each face. Secondly, I have a personal reason." Nado looked around and found the person he was seeking.

"Azurie, I now understand what you meant by ambitions. Your strength in turning away from life's pleasures and staying true to your beliefs is admirable." Upon hearing her name, Azurie looked around to find who was speaking. When she saw him, she was genuinely surprised. She acknowledged Nado with a nod of her head and a beautiful smile - the same smile Nado had thought about during his time away. "I won't take up any more of your time, but I'd like to invite each of you to a barbecue this Saturday at the park. It's all free, and you can bring as many friends as you'd like. I simply want to give back a little. You won't want to miss it." With that, Nado sat down, and the speaker began their speech.

Azurie didn't hear a word her father said after Nado finished speaking. She was still in shock. Nado was the last person she would have expected to see. Azurie had spent many nights crying, wrestling with herself, and questioning whether her faith was worth giving up the pleasures that other teenagers enjoyed. And yet, once again, Allah had provided her with an answer. Azurie recalled a particular scripture she read when feeling confused or uncertain - Surah 10 Ayat 109: "And follow, whatever is revealed to you, and remain patient until Allah brings forth His judgment. He is the best of those who judge." Allah is good, she thought as everyone stood to leave the mass.

Nado waited outside for Azurie, growing nervous as she exited the building and walked toward him. He knew exactly what he wanted to say, and as she approached him, his mouth began to shape the first word. A gentle hand on his shoulder interrupted his train of thought. Nado turned around to find himself face-to-face with Minister Malik Shakur, Azurie's father.

"As-Salaam-Alaikum, my brother," the minister said. "It was nice to have you with us, even if only for a short while. I also enjoyed your speech, but you know, anyone can make a speech. Politicians are especially good at it, mostly to gain votes. In your case, I hope that's not your goal." With that, Minister Shakur turned and walked away.

Nado understood the message clearly. He recognized the man as a minister but also as a father. Nado's thoughts returned to the present when he heard a voice he hadn't encountered in a year—yet he recognized it instantly. He turned to see Azurie looking as beautiful as ever, her captivating smile taking him back to their early morning encounter at McDonald's.

"I didn't think we'd cross paths again," said Azurie. "Neither did I," replied Nado. "I just wanted to ask if you'd let me escort you to the barbecue on Saturday. I know our last conversation didn't end well, and I'm not here to force my way back into your life. All I ask is for the honor of taking you to the barbecue. That's it." Nado gazed at Azurie, waiting patiently as she considered his invitation.

Azurie asked, "What kind of work do you do?" Nado smiled. "As I mentioned earlier, I've been away for a year and just returned home today. But I can assure you that my work will not be the same as before."

"What time is it?" inquired Azurie. Nado glanced at his diamond-studded Rolex watch. "No, no," she laughed, "I meant the barbecue. What time is the barbecue?" Nado's face flushed with embarrassment as he realized his mistake.

"Oh, it starts at 10 in the morning. It'll be really special, and I want you to join me." Azurie looked towards her parents, who were waiting by the car. She retrieved a pen from her purse and scribbled down a number. "Call me beforehand so I can be ready," she said, smiling at Nado before walking towards her awaiting parents.

Nado watched her until she entered the car and waved as they drove off. Everything was going according to plan. He had been free for less than 24 hours and had already set in motion all that he'd intended to do. As he walked, Nado thought about Saturday and Azurie. Yes, everything was unfolding perfectly.

———

CHAPTER SEVEN

Converging Paths: Shadows of the Past

As the young woman strolled down the bustling sidewalk, her focus honed in on a single desire: to satisfy that insatiable craving for a high. The world around her seemed to fade, a busy sidewalk full of people. Despite the crowd, she was cocooned in her own urgency. Her attempts to reach her source had hit a wall – unanswered calls echoing her frustration. Unlike the street- crack addicts, she had always moved in a different circle, shielded by a protector of sorts, sparing her the gritty grind others endured. But now, in this moment, that safety net felt distant.

Frustration mounted as her yearning intensified step by step. She knew a place, a refuge for her needs, yet uncertainty clouded her mind. Who would she encounter there? Familiar faces, perhaps? But did it really matter? A notion settled in – a belief that her drug use might enhance her appeal to men. With determination, just a few blocks separated her from the destination, her craving propelling her forward.

Meanwhile, Nado had been walking in a trance, lost in thoughts about Azurie. When he looked up, he was surprised to find himself in his old neighborhood - the place where he, his mother, and his sister had lived before he entered the drug game and moved them out. It was astonishing how things had changed yet remained the same. He noticed people still darting behind cars and recognized some guys who used to run errands for the dope dealers. His gaze shifted towards a dumpster, where an old man appeared to be standing.

Drawing closer, Nado's voice broke the air – an interruption to the person's solitude. The encounter held an uncanny weight, a glimpse into the intricacies of a world he thought he'd escaped. He had an idea that he had seen the person before. Nado approached the dumpster cautiously, stopping just short of the individual with their back turned. "Excuse me," said Nado. Startled, the person whirled around with surprising speed, holding a crowbar high above their head.

"Come on, and get it, sonny. If you don't want the rats eating on your ass, then you best be on your way," the man said. Nado replied, "I'm sorry, sir. I just thought I recognized you. Aren't you the man I see at McDonald's?" The man appeared puzzled by Nado's question but didn't lower his crowbar one inch.

"Say I wuz. What has it got to do with you sneaking up on me? A fella can get dey head torn up mighty bad sneaking up on people like dat." Nado replied, "I'm sorry. I didn't mean to sneak up on you. I'm a friend of Azurie." The mention of the name Azurie caused the crowbar to drop a few inches.

"I've seen you at McDonald's with her. She said you were her special friend," Nado stated. The man inquired, "You know Zurie, do you?" Nado reassured him, "Yes, sir. You can put your crowbar down. I'm not here to hurt you." Slowly, the man lowered the crowbar and slid it back into the sleeve of his dirty coat.

"You can't be too careless out hea, sonny. You got a lot of crazy folks running around dese days. Dey got all that new kind of dope dats making these people go crazy. Hell, I had one jest de other day, walk right up to me and tell me to give him my coat. Now you tell me, what in the hell can he do with this hea coat? You know what I gid him?"

The old man patted his coat sleeve where he had his crowbar hidden. "I gid him a light tap, side his noggin with old buster hea. He changed his mind about wanting my coat. I remember back in the days when a man could take a good drink of shine and feel good. Made you sit down on your ass too. I don't know what kind of shit dey got now. Make a mama sell her baby. Make a man sell his wife. It's crazy, man."

Nado replied, "I understand exactly where you're coming from." He noticed the old man's gaze and asked, "What's wrong? Why are you looking at me like that?" The old man responded, "I know you too. You used to be one of those dope sellers. Use to drive that little sporty black car around. I used to see you. I watch everyone – it's part of my survival to watch and listen."

The old man's words gave Nado an idea. "How would you like to earn a few dollars?" he asked. The old man looked at Nado before answering, "I don't sell no dope; I sell cans."

"No, no, it's not like that," Nado assured, reaching for his back pocket. The old man's arm moved suddenly, and like magic, a crowbar appeared in his hand. "Wait, I'm just getting my wallet. I want to show you a picture," explained Nado. He retrieved his wallet and drew out a photo of Necy. "Have you seen her before?"

The old man studied the picture for a moment and shook his head. "Naw, can't say I seen her before. Say, what is this picture stuff all about?" Nado replied, "That's my sister. I was in prison for a year, and during my absence, she began associating with the wrong crowd. She got involved with drugs, and I want to find out who she is getting it from so I can protect her." The old man gazed at Nado and shook his head.

"Looks like to me that you are getting back what you put out. You know the good Lord don't like ugly," the old man said. He turned his back on Nado and resumed digging through the dumpster. Nado realized he couldn't simply linger, waiting to find those who had supplied drugs to his sister. He also knew this old man was observant and aware of his surroundings. If anyone could uncover the information he sought, Nado believed it would be this watchful elder.

"What do you say about the job?" The old man continued to dig through the trash, seemingly ignoring Nado's question. After a moment of sifting through what appeared to be old clothes, the old man finally turned and faced Nado. "Sonny, ain't heard you offer no job yet. Ain't seen you do nuttin' but show dat der picher you say is your sister."

"I need you to keep your eyes open and see if you can spot my sister hanging out with anyone," said Nado. The old man replied, "Dats all you want me to do, just keep my eyes open?" Nado responded, "That's it. That's all I need from you. I'll even leave a picture so you can remember what she looks like."

The old man replied, "I may be old, sonny, but I ain't no dummy. What happened to your sister Chin?" Nado was puzzled by the question the old man had just asked him. "There is nothing wrong with her chin," said Nado. "Hasn't she had stitches in her chin before?" the old man asked. Nado thought for a moment, then realized what had just taken place. He looked at the picture he held in his hand and, after examining it closely, noticed the faint trace where stitches had once been on his sister's chin.

Nado couldn't help but smile. He reached into his pocket, took out a $100 bill, and gave it to the old man. This old man was sharper than Nado had given him credit for. "I'll give you a bonus if you can get me the information. Here is my number where you can reach me," Nado said as he handed the man a card with his number on it. Nado turned and started walking away. After a few steps, he stopped and turned back towards the old man, who was still standing there, admiring the $100 bill that Nado had given him.

"Hey there, you never told me your name," said Nado. The old man took a moment to look up and replied, "Everybody calls me 2-4, but my name is Dan." He immediately returned his attention to his $100 bill. Nado reminded him, "Hey, 2-4, don't forget to treat Azurie." The old man didn't look up but simply smiled, as he had already planned to do so.

As Nado walked on, heading for the cab station, his mind was so full of thoughts that he failed to notice the young lady who stood at the phone booth.

The phone continuously rang, frustrating Necy. She wondered where Boss Player could possibly be. Suddenly, her thoughts were interrupted by a distinct scent that signaled one thing - her brother's presence or the presence of someone with expensive taste. Necy slowly turned around and caught sight of her brother walking past the phone booth. She swiftly hung up the phone and hurriedly went in the opposite direction.

Necy was familiar with her surroundings, as this was her old stomping ground. She hurriedly walked down the sidewalk, passing the old man who was once again rummaging through the dumpster. Needing to get off the street for a while, she glanced up and noticed the sign of a little coffee shop. Without hesitation, she entered the shop and chose a table in a secluded corner, hoping to avoid being noticed by anyone, particularly Nado.

"I hope you understand the risks involved in the decision you're about to make. I'm not saying people can't change, but it's difficult to settle for less when you're used to the best. You've never let me down in anything you've done before, which is why I trust you now. Allah will provide guidance. Always remember, when faced with the truth, you must be strong and accept it." Azurie smiled at her father, saying, "It's just a barbecue, Daddy. He didn't ask me to marry him." She hugged her father tightly and added, "Your little girl knows how to stay away from bad boys. Remember, you were the one who taught me well." Minister Shakur smiled back and returned his daughter's hug. After all, worrying was his responsibility as a father. Azurie then proceeded to her room.

At the Dexter's house, Mrs. Nell tiptoed to the door and pressed her ear against it, but there was nothing to hear. At least Necy is finally getting some rest, she thought to herself. Eagerly awaiting Nado's arrival so she could rest too, she silently retreated from Necy's door and sat on the chair to keep a vigilant watch over her sleeping daughter. The jingling of keys roused Mrs. Nell as Nado opened the front door. She stood up and walked towards Nado.

"How is Necy?" Nado inquired. Mrs. Nell replied, "She's asleep in her room. My poor baby needs some rest. What can we do to help her, Nado?" "First, I need to figure out what's happening with her. Then, we'll determine the kind of assistance she needs. Let's get some sleep, and I'll talk to her tomorrow," Nado suggested. He kissed his mother's cheek, escorted her to her bedroom, and wished her goodnight. Mrs. Nell nodded, smiling, and entered her room. Nado retreated to his room and began reading his Quran. Mrs. Nell prayed fervently for the well-being of her family.

Necy observed every person and movement from within the booth. However, she wasn't the only one watching. King Kong occupied his usual spot, sipping black coffee and puffing on his signature Ashton cigars. He couldn't help but notice Necy as she rushed past his table toward the far corner. She appeared to be hiding from someone, he thought curiously. Her attractive look was somewhat familiar to King Kong, but he couldn't quite remember where he'd seen her before. As he contemplated this mystery and retrieved a mint from his pocket, Necy felt unnerved by this man's constant glances – she'd seen him converse with her brother Nado before his incarceration.

Necy pondered Boss Player once again. Why wouldn't he answer his phone? As her mind swirled with thoughts of Boss Player, King Kong approached the booth where Necy was seated. "Excuse me. Do you have company coming?" Kong stood before Necy with a smile, allowing her to examine the enormous gold and diamond ring adorning his finger. Instantly, Necy realized that this man was no ordinary individual. His posture and demeanor spoke volumes. "Play your cards right, Necy," she thought to herself. "Tonight, could be your lucky night."

"No, I don't have any company coming. Would you like to take a seat?" Necy offered. Kong grinned to himself. Bingo. "I have a better idea. How about we go for a drive? Enjoy the scenery and grab a few drinks or whatever floats your boat. What do you say to that?"

Here she was, just three minutes into meeting this man, and Necy was about to ride off with him, uncertain of what was to come. Well, she reasoned, it wouldn't have been any different with Boss Player. She might as well find out what this man was all about.

"Sure, why not?" Necy thought as she accepted Kong's extended hand. As they walked toward the door, Kong informed the man behind the counter that he would return later if anyone came looking for him. Outside, Kong courteously opened the door of his gold Mercedes-Benz 500 and allowed Necy to enter. After closing her door, Kong walked around the car with a smile. As they pulled onto the highway, Kong glanced at Necy once more; her face certainly reminded him of someone.

"What should I call you?" Kong asked. Necy pondered for a moment. She couldn't reveal her name, as there was a chance that Nado had mentioned her to him. Aware of an unspoken code among drug dealers barring them from involving each other's family members, she didn't want to create any issues. For now, all she needed was to get high. "Baby Boo," Necy finally said. "Everyone calls me Baby Boo."

"Baby Boo, I like that. So, what are you into, Baby Boo?" asked Kong. It all came down to her answer - either she'd get high or be taken back to the coffee shop. It was better to be upfront and save time. Necy hesitated before saying, "I like to get down." Silence followed her words as she awaited Kong's reaction. "Get down? What way do you get down?"

"I smoke. Occasionally, I do a little base. It excites me and sometimes makes me do things I wouldn't normally do. Just thinking about it makes me act strangely." Necy moved her hand up Kong's leg and didn't stop until she held his semi-hard penis. She felt him tremor when she started stroking him. Her doubts disappeared completely, and she smiled as they drove off into the night.

Nado woke up early the next morning and decided to make breakfast for his mother and sister. As he prepared the food, he thought about his sister's situation. She needed help to overcome her drug problem, and he believed that love and care from family could be the solution. With the breakfast tray in hand, Nado approached his mother's room and gently tapped on the door using his foot.

"Come in," his mother's soft voice responded. Nado explained that he needed help since his hands were full. His mother opened the door with a smile and reached out to assist him, but he refused, saying they would take the breakfast to Necy's room instead.

They crossed the hall to Necy's door, where Mrs. Nell knocked but received no answer. She knocked again, harder this time, but their knocks remained unanswered.

"Necy, Baby, wake up. We have something for you." There was no response. "Open the door, Mama," said Nado. Mrs. Nell's hand slowly grasped and turned the doorknob. Gradually, the door opened inward. Nado and his mother stood in the doorway, gazing at Necy's empty bed, which appeared untouched. They stared at the flowered curtains, waving gently as the breeze entered through the open window—the same window Necy had escaped from. Nado shook his head, glancing at his mother. Mrs. Nell stood motionless as tears of sorrow and pain streamed down her cheeks. Nado returned the breakfast to the kitchen; it was no longer their priority.

"Have you ever seen this girl before?" Boss Player stared at the photo Lil Boot handed him. Something felt off about the situation. Had the little bitch told them about him supplying her drugs? Boss Player couldn't confess now—regardless of what she had revealed, he had to deny knowing her.

"Naw, I can't say I've ever seen her before. Who is she anyway?" responded Boss Player. "She's going to be someone's worst nightmare. So, you're telling me you've never seen her before?" asked Lil Boot.

"I'm positive. You just asked me that, and I told you I've never seen her before," said Boss Player.

"And I'm telling you this. If I find out you are lying to me, I'll be back. Let's leave this place." After Lil Boot and JT Dollar had bounced out of Boss Player's place, Boss sank into his seat, inhaling a deep breath that seemed to deflate him. He knew that trouble was brewing. Why the hell did he mess with a drug dealer's sister? He realized he had violated the code when he began supplying her with drugs. Keeping his distance from her was now a no-brainer. How could he have been so incredibly foolish?

When Lil Boot handed him that photo, Boss's eyes zeroed in on the guy standing next to her, recognition sparking instantly. That dude had been the biggest dealer around before vanishing behind bars. Clearly, he was back and wanted someone to pay for supplying his sister with drugs. Boss knew full well they wouldn't rest until they unearthed the truth. The only thing left for him to be prepared for whatever came.

"What's up, Homie? What are you up to?" Lil Boot asked over the phone. "Necy sneaked out of the house, probably sometime last night. We checked on her this morning, and her bed hadn't even been slept in. I hope you have some good news," said Nado.

"We just left a guy named Boss Player's house. Slapped the pic of Necy in front of him, but he's swearing up and down he's never laid eyes on her," Lil Boot reported.

"What made you go to his house?" asked Nado. "Well, JT and I had a sit-down with him not long ago, talking' business, and he lets slip this gem about having a little honey who's down for anything. And we both know what that means. He's got someone deep in something that they weren't supposed to be doing," Lil Boot broke it down, his tone dripping with implication.

"Not necessarily," was Nado's response. "You have some girls who get down like that," he added. "Didn't I tell you that I had to go and meet him? I don't meet suckers to kick the Bo-Bo. Anyway, we rode off and decided to go by his place to see if we could get a look at this little honey. We cruised by his house and saw him with this fine-ass girl standing outside by his car. She didn't look like someone with bad habits at all. I just had this gut feeling that he knew something, so we checked on him again," said Lil Boot.

"How did he look when you showed him the picture?" asked Nado. "If you're asking if he gave himself away, no. We'll keep digging, though, and keep an eye open tonight." Nado inquired, "Have you made arrangements for the meat for the barbecue?"

"We'll handle all that Friday evening. I have a couple of people who are going to bring some big grills for us to use," replied Lil Boot. "I guess you guys can get ready to have some fun soon. Who knows, maybe the three of us can start a barbecue business." A moment of silence followed Nado's last words as he let the idea plant itself in Lil Boot's mind. "What are you guys doing right now?" asked Nado.

JT responded, "Well, nothing really. Why? What do you have planned? Come by here and pick me up. I need to drop by a few places and say hello to some of my old associates," said Nado. Ten minutes later, the three partners were riding out just like they used to do in the good old days. "Where should we park?" asked Lil Boot. "Let's go by the little coffee shop where we first began," suggested Nado, smiling to himself. Kong definitely wasn't going to like this if, in fact, he was still around.

"What's up with the coffee shop?" asked JT. "I just want to drop in on an old friend, that's all." They rode the rest of the way, discussing what had happened while Nado had been gone. Upon arriving at the little coffee shop, Nado noticed that

Kong's Mercedes was not in the parking lot. "Wait here for a moment; let me see if Kong is inside."

Nado got out of the car and entered the coffee shop. After learning that Kong had left only moments ago, he returned to the car. "Was he in there?" asked Lil Boot. "No, I just missed him by a few minutes."

"What's next?" asked JT. "Let's drop in on the spot," said Nado. JT gave Lil Boot a puzzled glance but remained silent. It didn't seem like Nado was trying to leave the game, in his eyes. Two destinations, two drug-related outcomes. JT wondered to himself, what was Nado up to? They quickly arrived at the spot, and despite the chaos, things were bustling. People were everywhere, and cars were coming and going.

As Nado and his companions made their way through the parking lot, those who seemed in a hurry slowed down either to greet them or to ask if the barbecue was still happening. Nado responded with a smile and even stopped to chat with a few acquaintances.

Even Lil Boot found it peculiar because Nado used to avoid associating with most people, especially those using drugs. Confused by Nado's behavior, Lil Boot and JT Dollar decided to distance themselves. This would allow them to observe Nado's actions more clearly and try to understand what was happening.

"Ah, man, isn't that Nado?" someone shouted. All eyes turned toward Nado as he slowly approached the group of hustlers. It felt just like old times. They all greeted Nado and those who hadn't known him before mentioned they had heard about his achievements in the game.

"I'm not here for that, fellas. I came to personally invite each of you to the barbecue on Saturday. It's going to be something special. Don't forget to bring your lady friends because they definitely won't want to miss it," said Nado. After leaving that spot, Nado and his crew visited several other hot spots where he extended the same personal invitation to attend the free barbecue.

"Man, I am tired," said Lil Boot. "You haven't seen tired yet, Master Chef," Nado smiled at Lil Boot. "Yeah, yeah, don't remind me," said Lil Boot. They continued riding around for a while longer, enjoying the scenery and each other's company. Nado started to contemplate the implications of the one-week deadline he had set for his partners.

"Have you guys given any thought to what I talked to you about the other day?" asked Nado. Neither of his partners answered immediately, as Nado knew this was a difficult decision for both of them. It had become their lifeline—the source that allowed them to live out their every dream.

Finally, JT spoke up. "Do you actually realize what you're asking us to give up, Nado? I mean, it's who we are now." "But what were you before, JT?" asked Nado. JT paused for a moment before responding. "I was one of us—one who went to different schools and exchanged old tennis shoes each week so people wouldn't know I only had one pair. One who used to wonder if there would be enough food at home for my siblings to eat. One who, with the only two partners I've ever had, took a chance and made it. That's what I was, and now this is who I am."

Nado's heart felt heavy after hearing JT's words, but he wouldn't let feelings and emotions interfere with his goals and objectives. "Look at me, JT," Nado said, waiting until JT focused on his face before continuing. "I, too, have lived the exact same life as you. So has Lil Boot. I can't force you to do anything you don't want to do, nor would I ever try to do that. You are my brother, and I love you. Have you ever gotten tired? I've gotten tired. I've had a good run and came out on top. You've had a good run—now it's your turn to come out on top." Lil Boot listened to the conversation between his partners attentively. If he hadn't believed it before, he knew now that Nado was serious about leaving the game behind them.

"Ever notice how what's right for you might be wrong for someone else? Your rock-solid beliefs might be quicksand to another person. Maybe you can keep riding that wave of certainty indefinitely, but why gamble when you can choose to walk away now? I admit I haven't explained myself fully, but in time, you'll understand where I stand and why. Let's go back to the coffee shop and see if Kong has returned," said Nado. Nado's words carried a mix of intrigue and mystery.

The journey back to the coffee shop was a quiet one, a road paved with individual thoughts. Just before they rolled into the parking lot, Nado's eyes locked onto the gleaming gold Mercedes, comfortably situated in its usual spot, intentionally distanced from other customers' cars. With a smirk, Nado said, "Looks like Kong has finally returned. Let's go say hello to our old friend."

What Nado didn't realize was that the complex network of relationships between his partners and Kong had gradually dissolved. During Nado's absence, Kong's attempt to hike up the prices for Lil Boot and JT hadn't gone over well. Instead of paying more, they turned to a savvy Cuban man they'd met who offered better prices than they'd initially gotten from Kong. This shrewd move allowed them to buy more at a cheaper rate and sell it at prices lower than Kong's.

In an unexpected twist, Lil Boot and JT Dollar had ascended to become the top distributors, relegating Kong's once-thriving supply to a dusty corner. Frustration-fueled actions followed as Kong dispatched his two toughest enforcers to bring them back in their place. Yet, these enforcers had limped back to Kong, one nursing a fractured arm and the other grinning a toothless grin, courtesy of Lil Boot and JT's spirited resistance.

Kong knew at that moment that Lil Boot and JT were forces to be reckoned with. They had confronted Kong in a crowded coffee shop, warning him not to come after them again. Ever since that day, he had left them alone. Now, they were about to meet face-to-face for the first time since the confrontation.

When Lil Boot and JT walked into the shop, they immediately caught the attention of the owner. He paused his glass cleaning and fixed his gaze on them. And he wasn't the only one. Kong, too, was watching them closely, anticipating potential problems. Despite this, he was resolved not to let these youngsters embarrass him as they had done in the past.

Kong discreetly moved his hand away from the table as Nado approached with a greeting. "Hello there, Kong. It's been a while." Nado offered his hand in greeting; it took Kong a moment to hide the small pistol between his legs before shaking hands.

"What brings you down here?" asked Kong cautiously, eyeing Lil Boot and JT Dollar. "I see you have your friends with you." For Lil Boot and JT, it was as if Kong had not said anything at all.

Nado replied, "I just wanted to personally invite you to our barbecue this Saturday. I assure you that it'll be a great time. I won't take up any more of your time; I know you're a busy man." He noticed Kong's puzzled expression as he looked once more at Lil Boot and JT before leaving.

"Hey, let's get out of here before I lose it," Lil Boot's words burst out, carrying an urgency that couldn't be ignored. Nado was confused and stunned - he couldn't comprehend what had gotten into Lil Boot. Without wasting time, he followed him, with JT close behind. As they left, a paper slipped from Nado's hand and went unnoticed by them.

However, Kong noticed the fallen paper and rose from his seat, and his curiosity piqued as he picked it up. There were no words to read - only a picture that left him breathless. It was a photo of Nado and the young woman now sleeping in his bed, who had introduced herself as Baby Boo. Kong recognized her face and recalled their past encounter. Smirking at the thought of payback, he returned to his table, keeping his eyes on the picture.

CHAPTER EIGHT

Redemption and Revelations

While working, Azurie's mind strayed far from her station. As she stood behind the cash register, her focus waned, overtaken by thoughts of Nado. Her eyes would drift towards the windows, silently hoping to catch a glimpse of Nado arriving. Lately, she had been staying at home on purpose, just in case Nado tried to contact her. This unspoken desire enveloped her like a shroud, weaving into her daily life a tale of eagerness and wishful thinking.

She smiled at the thought. At least he was being true to his word. He had told her he wouldn't pressure her into seeing him, and he hadn't tried. Lost in thought, she suddenly heard a familiar voice that brought her back to the present.

"Man! I don't know why you mess up my order every day." Azurie looked at Dan, giving him a welcome to Micky D's smile. "I apologize for the inconvenience, sir. Perhaps this will make up for your trouble." Azurie turned to the coffee pot and poured their largest cup. Handing it over, she apologized once more and mentioned the coffee was on the house. Dan, however, had other plans.

"Naw, that's alright. I'll keep what you give me, and I'll pay for the coffee," said Dan. He reached into his pocket and pulled out the hundred-dollar bill that Nado had given him. Azurie froze. Dan didn't miss her reaction and grinned. "Got me a little job. Private investigator," said Dan, noticing Azurie's increasing confusion when he attempted to hand her the hundred-dollar bill.

"I work independently, not for none of them companies. This fella just walked up to me out of the blue and showed me a picture if-in I ever seen her. Told me if-in I do, just call him up. I git a bonus if-in I can find her. I ain't seen her yet. This hea is mine even if-in I don't find her. No strings hooked on it. Well, one odd thing though: he tolt me to buy you lunch. Nice looking young fella. What you say about lunch?" Said Dan

"You don't know this man's name? Why is he looking for the girl, and who did he say she was?" asked Azurie. "Sho, I know who hired me to find her. He said that wuz his sista, and she done gone and got herself on that dope. Anyway, what about that lunch?" "Mr. Dan, you need the money more than I need to be taken out to lunch. Why don't you save your money, and the coffee is still on the house," said Azurie. "Well, if-in that's what you want, I can't make you go. Jest make sho if-in one ask you to tell them, I did." Dan took the coffee and turned to leave. "What makes you think I'll see this man?" Azurie asked. Dan didn't stop walking as he responded, "It's jest a feeling, Zuri – jest a feeling."

"Hey, what was that all about?" asked Nado after they had gotten into the car and driven out of the parking lot. "What made you go off like that?" Nado looked at Lil Boot as he waited for his answer. He could see how Lil Boot was fighting with himself to maintain control.

Finally, JT responded to Nado's question. "We had a little run-in with Kong while you were gone. He tried to raise the prices on us, but we found another supplier that was cheaper than what we were originally paying. So, we stopped dealing with him. He got upset and sent his goons after us; we sent them back to him a little bruised up and stepped down on him. We haven't gone near him until today."

Nado understood now. He knew his partners would never allow anyone to put them down. "I kind of figured that after I left, he would try something. Anyway, very soon, we won't have to worry about those kinds of problems. Are you guys hungry?"

As they approached McDonald's, Nado thought it would be a good opportunity to both grab a bite to eat and say hello to Azurie. "Yeah," said Lil Boot, already knowing why Nado asked, "Let's get something to eat." He turned on his blinker so the car behind could back off and avoid rear-ending them. Pulling into the parking lot, Nado spotted Dan about to leave through a small pathway. Jumping out of the still-moving car, Nado called out, "2-4!" Dan recognized the voice and turned around.

"Good morning," said Nado. "Any luck? I haven't heard from you yet." Dan sipped his coffee before replying, "Ain't seen her yet, but I'm on the job. Don't you worry yourself nun. I got a bonus cumin to me dat I got to git." He grinned as Nado placed his hand on Dan's shoulder. "I'll find you another job as well," Nado assured him.

Changing the subject, Nado asked about Dan's plans for Saturday. "Well, I'll be doing the same old thang that I've always been doing. It's a little different now." Dan replied cryptically. Puzzled, Nado listened as Dan said, "That wuz Rick James, man. Don't you know nothing about Fire and Desire?" The two laughed together, and for a moment, Nado felt as if he'd found a father figure he never had.

Nado asked if Dan could help with his barbecue on Saturday. As Dan began to look downcast, Nado quickly added that there was only one catch: all helpers had to wear specific clothing that he would provide. "Don't forget, you'll get paid for your time." Hearing this, Dan lifted his head and looked at Nado.

"You sure know how to use words without so-in not to hurt nobody's feelings," said Dan. Nado should have known that he couldn't fool Dan. "I just want to help. Don't think for a second that I pity you because I don't. Your life has been a thousand times harder than mine, and you're still standing strong. That doesn't deserve pity." Once again, Dan understood the unspoken and smiled. "What do you say?" asked Nado.

"When do I get my clothes?" Nado took note of Dan's clothes and shoe size and told him to meet back at 6 p.m. Dan walked away whistling to himself, proud of securing two jobs in two days - one as an investigator and another as a master chef. Before venturing too far, Dan turned back and shouted, "I offered to buy Zurie lunch, but she told me to treat myself to something nice." With that, he continued on his way.

Azurie looked up in surprise as Nado and two guys she had first seen him with walked through the door. Nado smiled at her and approached the counter. "Welcome to McDonald's. May I take your order, please?"

"Good morning, Azurie. We'll have three number threes with orange juice. How have you been doing since we last spoke?" asked Nado. "I'm doing fine, Nado. How about you?" said Azurie. Nado responded, "I'm kind of tired from all the running around I've been doing. I've got a lot more ground to cover before the big day tomorrow. You haven't had second thoughts, have you?"

"No, to be honest, I've been looking forward to it," she gave Nado a playful smile. Nado agreed, "I've been looking forward to it too. Is your father going to attend?"

"He wouldn't miss a free barbecue for the world. Are you in a hurry? I have something that I would like to talk to you about," said Azurie. "I could never be too busy where I don't have time to listen to someone. Is there something wrong?" asked Nado.

"I don't know. Let me go and get someone to relieve me for a few minutes." Azurie handed Nado their orders and, after giving him his change, went to the back and got someone to cover for her. Nado watched as Azurie walked toward where he and his partners were sitting. He had left a seat open beside him, but it was evident that she wanted to speak privately when she didn't sit down.

Nado was about to stand up when Azurie began to speak. "The manners of some people... My name is Azurie," she said as she extended a hand towards Lil Boot. She looked at Nado, smiling as he continued to rise from his chair. Nado said, "I apologize. I've never formally introduced you, have I? Azurie, these are the best friends a person could ever have the pleasure of knowing." Nado pointed at Lil Boot. "This is Lil Boot, and my other partner is JT Dollar. Fellas, this is Azurie." They shook hands and sat back down, eager to return to their breakfast yet patient enough not to be rude.

"I don't want to be rude, but I only have a few moments, and I really need to talk to your friend," said Azurie, smiling. Nado returned her smile with a slightly saddened one. "Would you excuse us for a moment, please?" Azurie asked. Lil Boot and JT nodded, diving back into their food as soon as Nado and Azurie walked away.

In the far corner of the restaurant, Nado waited for Azurie to take her seat before sitting down. He sat back and waited for her to speak. Collecting her thoughts, Azurie asked, "Do you remember the first time we met?" "Of course, Azurie. How could I forget that day?" replied Nado. She smiled and continued, "Do you remember the old man who you said was trying to cheat me out of free food?" Nado knew what she was thinking now and momentarily feared she might strike him again over the ambitious tip incident.

"Sure, I remember him. Has he been harassing you again? If I'm not mistaken, I think I saw him leaving as we were pulling in," said Nado. He made a quick motion to get up, hoping to catch the man before he got too far. However, Azurie's expression displayed fear as she grabbed Nado's arm, pulling him back down into his seat.

"No, no, it's nothing like that. He is a very nice man," Azurie said as she collected her thoughts. "It's just, I don't know. Maybe it's nothing; maybe I'm jumping to conclusions. Maybe I shouldn't have bothered you with this."

"What is it, Azurie? Don't you trust my judgment? Do you believe people can change and work a legitimate job?" Nado asked. "Oh, I'm sorry, Nado, if I gave you that impression. I never meant to do that. When someone tries to show their gratitude, it would be nice if you would accept it," Azurie replied.

Azurie didn't like how the conversation had gone. Instead of confiding in someone as she thought she was about to, she found herself on the receiving end of a reprimand. She didn't appreciate being scolded, especially by someone she barely knew.

"Now, you just hold on a second," Azurie said, raising her voice. Nado noticed he had touched a nerve and inwardly smiled at how her pretty smile had been replaced by a less cheerful one.

"No, you hold on. You asked to talk to me. Evidently, Dan has done something you don't like," Nado countered. Azurie's expression shifted suddenly. "Just because you've always helped him doesn't mean he can't get a job and invite you out for lunch," Nado explained without revealing too much.

Nado sat back and smiled when understanding registered on Azurie's face. "So, are you the one who gave him that money?" she asked. "Gave? No, not gave - he's earning that money by doing me a very important favor. No, it's nothing illegal. You see, there is good in everyone," Nado clarified.

Azurie took his hand in hers and said, "Thank you so much. I didn't want to believe that he had done something wrong. It just surprised me to see him with that kind of money. I know it wasn't a lot, but seeing him with it was truly a surprise."

"Guess what he told me?" Azurie started laughing. "He said he was a private investigator hired by a man to find a missing girl," Azurie continued. "Who is she, Nado?" Nado reached into his back pocket and pulled out his wallet. He looked inside several times but remained silent. "What's wrong, Nado?" asked Azurie.

Nado checked his shirt pocket and found it empty. "I had a picture of her, but I seem to have misplaced it. She's my sister," Nado explained the situation to Azurie. When he finished, he noticed Azurie was gripping his hand tightly as if trying to share some pain he must have been feeling. He quickly changed the subject.

"2-4, I mean Dan, has another job tomorrow helping at the barbecue. I need to get him something to wear. Do you know where Dan lives?" asked Nado. Azurie's face appeared sad once more.

"I don't think he has a place to stay. I need to get back to work. Thank you again," said Azurie. She leaned over and gave Nado a gentle kiss on the cheek before strolling back behind the counter. Nado sat in the corner thinking about her, realizing she was the kind of person with whom he could live his life and be content. He eventually got up and walked back to join his partners.

"Ready to roll? We got a lot of shopping to do and not much time to do it,'" said Nado. Nado waved goodbye to Azurie as he and his partners walked through the door. He motioned to her that he would call her, and she nodded her head to let him know that it would be fine. Azurie went back to work, feeling better than she had felt in a very long time. Back on her face was the beautiful smile that she always greeted everyone with.

Mrs. Nell slowly walked around Necy's room, taking in the quiet and peaceful atmosphere. As she turned towards the dresser, her eyes fell upon a photo that brought tears to her eyes. The picture featured a young Necy and Nado playfully piled on top of Mrs. Nell.

Despite her exhaustion after work, she always found the energy to wrestle with them until they were all tired, sometimes cuddling together just like in this photo and falling asleep on the floor. She picked up the picture and sat on the edge of Necy's bed, her heart aching for the little girl who had once been her baby. Alone in the serene room, Mrs. Nell rocked back and forth while gazing at the photo, tears of sadness streaming down her cheeks.

Nado and his friends focused on their last-minute preparations. They had visited a local store specializing in creating family reunion shirts and collected an order of T-shirts. Their next stop was the supermarket – a place Nado knew well since his mother had always shopped there. He recalled how he would sprint to this same store, grasping his mom's grocery list, stretching on his tiptoes just to place it on the countertop.

Of course, he never carried any money with him. He had always assumed that the small, black-haired man with white strands was just being kind, but later discovered that his mother worked hard to pay for everything he received from him. Every two weeks, she would go to the store herself and settle the bills.

Now, he stood in front of the same man who appeared not to have aged a day.

"I want to thank you for getting all this meat at a wholesale price for me, Mr. Early D. I would have spent much more than this $20,000," said Nado. "You're welcome, son. Your mama has been good to me for a long time. I was happy to help you out. I just want to know one thing: why did you spend all your money on meat for people you don't know?" asked Mr. Early.

"It's a long story, Mr. Early D. I'll stop by one day and tell you all about it. Don't forget to come and get some of this meat tomorrow; it's not every day that you get to sell someone meat and then eat some of it for free."

Nado thanked him once more before he and his partners carried the meat outside and loaded it into the car. "I'll take my half and store it in my mom's freezer until tomorrow. You two split up the rest." Lil Boot drove Nado home and helped him store the meat they had purchased.

"I'll hit you guys up later," said Nado.

Nado walked down the hall and paused outside his sister's room. The house was quiet, and he wondered if his sister had returned and was now resting peacefully in her bed. He exhaled, reached for the knob, turned it slowly, and gently pushed the door open.

What he saw nearly brought tears to his eyes. He stood in the doorway, watching his mother's trembling figure as she clutched a baby picture of him and his sister. Silently, Nado closed the door, retrieved his car keys from the rack, and headed to the garage. He started up the Beamer and drove off, determined to find his sister not only for his mother but also for himself.

Inside Kong's house, Necy sifted through a closet shelf, grappling with a tangled string in hopes of uncovering a hidden cache of drugs. Her initial search seemed futile, but she eventually unearthed a valuable stash hidden within Kong's closet. The sight of the neatly bundled cash made her heart beat uncontrollably. A single glance confirmed its worth. Immediately, she called a cab, leaving Kong's front door wide open.

Necy stepped out of the taxi, handing the fare to the driver. She was consumed by remorse, having stolen Kong's money but unable to fulfill the promise she had made. As her restlessness intensified, she realized that a quick high might alleviate her unease. With only one hurdle left—procuring what she sought after—she embarked on her journey, wandering without any particular direction, uncertain of her next move. Now facing only one obstacle—finding what she needed—she began wandering aimlessly, unsure of where to go.

Upon returning home, Kong found both Baby Boo and a stash of cash from his closet gone. A thorough search confirmed that nothing else was missing. Unyielding, Kong departed the house once more, intent on giving Baby Boo a harsh lesson in street wisdom. Regardless of her female gender, she would face consequences.

2-4 had been scouring the local hotspots all morning while working on his new investigator job. Despite his efforts, he hadn't achieved any success yet. As evening approached and he considered moving to a different location, 2-4 noticed a group of young boys crowding around a man displaying a photo. He moved closer to see what had captured their attention. Just as he got into position for a better view, one of the boys shouted, "What the fuck do you want, old man?"

2-4 turned to face the boy, who was no older than 15 or 16. Instead of escalating the situation, he lowered his head and walked away. Frustrated, Kong offered a reward for information about the girl shown in the picture.

Nado pulled up alongside 2-4 and honked his horn. "What's up, 2-4? I've got something for you." 2-4 glanced around before approaching Nado's car. "Come on, get in," urged Nado. He could see the hesitation in 2-4's expression as he stood next to the car. "It's okay, hop in," said Nado, reaching over to open the door. Reluctantly, 2-4 got in, and Nado grabbed a small duffel bag. It contained the clothes Nado had promised, along with an electric razor and other toiletries.

"I brought the things you'll need for tomorrow. Where are you planning to clean up?" asked Nado. A sad expression crossed 2-4's face as he replied, "I know just the place. Close the door before you fall out." After 2-4 closed the door, Nado drove off.

As they rode together, Nado couldn't help but notice the pungent odor emanating from 2-4. He pulled into a motel parking lot and stopped next to the office. "Wait here — I'll be right back," said Nado. He left briefly before returning to open 2-4's door.

"Here's your key to your room," Nado told him. He took the bag from 2-4 and walked with him to the door. "Go ahead and open it." 2-4 inserted the key into the lock and opened the door, revealing all sorts of clothing and shoes scattered everywhere inside. There was a pile of undergarments, T-shirts, and several pairs of socks lying on the bed.

"It's all yours. The rent is paid up until the end of the month. I know we don't really know each other, but I think you'd make a good partner. I want you to practice proper hygiene and become the person you once were," said Nado. He was flooded with emotions as he saw a tiny tear roll down 2-4's face.

"It's been a long time since someone eva did summin for me. You don't know how much it means," replied 2-4. He wiped his eyes with his dirty coat sleeve and stared at all the new clothes Nado had bought him.

"Well, I've got a lot to do. Clean yourself up and rest because we have plenty of work tomorrow. If you happen to go out, keep an eye out for my sister," Nado said. They still hadn't seen or heard from her. Without saying another word, Nado turned and walked out the door.

Necy had walked until her feet grew tired. She found a secluded spot and sat down. Unfortunately, she didn't get a chance to rest her aching feet as a homeless man appeared out of nowhere. "What Chu got?" He looked directly at Necy as he slowly approached her. Fear of what was about to happen brought Necy quickly to her feet. Without thinking, she clutched her purse and easily dodged the homeless man before finding herself back on the busy streets.

Necy ran without thinking about her destination. When she finally slowed down, she realized she had traveled quite a distance. A couple more blocks would take her to her childhood neighborhood. She needed to find a place to go. That's when she remembered the money in her purse and noticed the motel sign. Necy smiled, quickly walking toward the motel office.

Nado departed from the motel, leaving 2-4 to carry on with his investigation. He steered towards the projects, his former home with his mother and sister. Parking his car, he embarked on a search, hopeful to either spot his younger sister or glean clues about her location.

Freddie was just leaving his room, having met an addict nearby, and brought her to the motel for some fun. As he walked across the parking lot, he noticed a girl in the office. At first, he casually glanced at her but soon stopped to take a better look. Surprised, Freddie covertly moved closer to a parked car, using it as cover while anticipating the girl's next move.

He didn't have to wait long; the girl exited the office and went straight to a room in the far corner of the motel. Freddie approached the door and checked the room number before heading back in excitement.

However, Freddie wasn't the only one who had noticed the girl entering the room; another observant man was also watching. 2-4 quickly grabbed the phone and dialed the number Nado had left him, anxiety mounting as he awaited a response. The voice on the other end greeted, "Hello, this is Nell." Unfortunately, Nado wasn't home. 2-4 thought to himself that the voice he heard on the phone sounded familiar.

"Hello. This is Kong." Freddie panted into the phone. "I got her, I got her," said Freddie. Kong responded, "You got who? What are you talking about?"

"That girl, man. The one whose picture you showed us today. I know where she is," said Freddie. This caught Kong's attention.

"You said you'd pay, right? Well, I found what you were looking for," Freddie announced. "Where is she? Tell me before she gets away," Kong demanded, eager to locate her.

It wasn't just the money on his mind; he wanted to use her to get back at those who had betrayed him. "What about my pay?" asked Freddie.

"You'll get paid! Now tell me where she is," Kong insisted. "How do I know you won't take her and forget your promise?" inquired Freddie. Annoyed but desperate, Kong had no choice but to agree.

"I'll tell you what - I'll leave your payment with Red Ball at the coffee shop. How does that sound?" replied Kong.

The line went silent as Freddie considered the offer. "Do you know who I am? The reward I offered for this information doesn't mean shit to me; I've got bitches who blow more than that in 30 minutes!" boasted Kong.

"Okay, I'll tell you. Go to the motel on Peachtree Avenue, and she will be in room two," said Freddie. "I'm on my way was all he could get out before the line went dead." Kong rushed out the door to his car, got the money, took it back inside, and gave it to Red Bull.

"Someone will come by shortly. Give this to him." With that, Kong turned and rushed through the door.

Nado was in receipt of a corresponding message from his trusted investigator. As he prepared to engage a group of men, 2-4 swiftly caught up to him. He informed Nado that he had seen Necy entering the same motel where he was staying, located down the street.

Nado bolted without a second thought, darting across the street without checking for traffic. His sudden appearance nearly triggered a collision as a car swerved to avoid hitting him. The car screeched to a halt, its tires squealing under the intense pressure. The bumper struck Nado's leg, throwing him off balance, yet he kept his eyes firmly ahead. He could see the motel's flashing lights up ahead - just one more block to go.

Nado absorbed the impact and dashed on, darting through the intersection into the motel parking lot. The driver, taken aback, had to gather himself. He'd seen a figure rushing towards the intersection but was too engaged with the motel's flashing sign. It was only after his car's bumper hit Nado that his focus shifted.

The driver had hit Nado with substantial force and anticipated him to tumble, but he was mistaken. Nado merely stumbled and briefly turned, offering a fleeting view of his face. The driver now observed as Nado sprinted across the motel lot, bee-lining for the very room he'd intended to visit.

Nado felt his leg throb where the car had struck him. He knew he should tend to it later – for now, he had to reach his sister Necy before she slipped away. Breathless, he came to a halt right in front of Necy's rented room and hammered on the door repeatedly.

Necy was just settling in after an exhausting run across town. As she reached for the phone to contact Boss Player, a thunderous noise from the door startled her, causing her to lose balance and knock over a lamp. With the sudden silence that followed, Necy lay on the floor, eyes fixed on the door.

"Open the door, Necy. I know you're in there," her brother's voice called out, leaving her in shock. How could he have found her so quickly? She realized she had been holding her breath and let out a sigh of relief.

Breathless and still on the floor, she tried not to make a sound. Her brother continued, "Listen, Necy, damn it! I love you; Mama loves you. We know you're going through a tough time right now, but we want to help you. It's too hard for you to face this alone. Open the door; let's sit down and talk – just the two of us."

Nado stood outside the door, waiting patiently for her response. Her brother's words cut into her like a knife. She knew without a doubt that Nado was right. She was no longer the same person, and her drug use was undoubtedly the reason why. She had to make a choice soon, as she knew she could never survive on the streets. Reflecting on why she came to this room in the first place, she began to stand up.

"Necy, I'm not going anywhere. If I have to stay here until you decide to come out, then I will," said Nado. Not wanting her brother to wait outside any longer, Necy got up and slowly walked to the door, opening it. On the other side stood Nado with an anxious expression and a smile.

"I'm sorry, Nado. I'm so sorry," Necy said as tears streamed down her face. Nado quickly approached his sister and gently wrapped his arms around her, softly stroking her hair as he whispered into her ear. "It's okay, Necy. Everything is going to be alright now. You just have to be strong, and we'll get through this together." Together, Nado and his sister walked back into the motel room.

Kong sat in his car, observing the scene before him. It was evident that Nado had someone watching his sister as well. If the guy who called Kong hadn't been so difficult, he would have reached the room before Nado. A terrible confrontation might have unfolded that night. He realized he would just have to bide his time. Kong smiled to himself, thinking, "You're not in the clear yet, my little one; you're definitely not in the clear." He then started his car and drove away.

2-4 had been listening through his slightly open door, and he knew he had done his job well. Nado was now with his sister in the room. Closing the door, 2-4 started going through the items Nado had given him to prepare for his new job tomorrow. He turned and walked towards the bathroom, the anticipation of a warm shower and a moment of relaxation fueling his steps. It had been an eternity since he had luxuriated in such a simple pleasure, but he intended to enjoy every second.

Switching on the shower to check if it worked, 2-4 removed his dingy clothes and stepped under the steady flow of water – instantly feeling his whole body relax. After thoroughly cleansing himself, 2-4 approached the mirror, gazing at the reflection that stared back at him. Months of unshaven neglect had obscured the face he once knew so well. Yet, this was about to change.

Utilizing the electric razor, Nado had left on the sink counter, 2-4 plugged it in and switched it on. With a steady hand and deliberate strokes, he carefully sheared off the stubborn hair, layer by layer. He now saw in the mirror a man he used to know – someone who meant something to many people. This reflection inspired 2-4 to be that man again. "A haircut, that's what I need now," he thought.

With a renewed spirit burning within him, 2-4 groomed himself further and put on fresh clothes. Finally, he left through the door with a tightly sealed garbage bag containing dirty, smelly clothes that would never be worn again.

As he walked toward the dumpster, he noticed a young couple holding each other close, strolling through the parking lot. The man glanced his way but didn't acknowledge him. At that moment, 2-4 knew he could reclaim his former self. Eager to get his haircut, he hurried toward the hood.

———

CHAPTER NINE

Return and Realization

Mrs. Nell sat in front of the TV, unfocused on its sight and sound. She was about to pour her third cup of coffee when the phone rang. After the third ring, she picked it up— "Hello, this is Nell speaking."

"Hey, mama, this is Nado. Do you have anything cooked?"

"Not yet, but I can if you're hungry. When are you coming home?" Mrs. Nell asked.

"I'm on my way right now with company. I think they'll be hungry too." Mrs. Nell inquired, "My baby? Did you find her?"

"Yes, mama. We'll be home shortly," said Nado before hanging up.

Mrs. Nell stood for a moment with the phone next to her ear before realizing she should be preparing food for her baby girl's return. Twenty minutes later, Nado led Necy through the door as Mrs. Nell dropped what she was doing and lovingly embraced her daughter in a warm hug.

"It's going to be alright, sweetie. You're home now," said Mrs. Nell. Nado suggested, "Take her to shower while I finish preparing the meal." Necy followed her mother down the hallway and into the bathroom. After showering and eating, Nado guided her to her bedroom, where they sat on the bed and talked until exhaustion took over.

Nado gently lifted her head off his shoulder, laying her down on the bed. He sat for a moment, gazing at his sleeping sister, and acknowledged his own weariness.

Nado removed his shoes and stretched out beside Necy, draping his arm across her stomach. As a light sleeper, he knew if she tried to sneak away, she would have to carefully maneuver out from under his protective arm.

Before long, both siblings were sound asleep. Mrs. Nell peeked into their room and found them both resting peacefully. Determined to prevent Necy from escaping again, she placed a chair near the bed and tenderly grasped Necy's hand in hers. In no time, she, too, drifted off to sleep, holding gently onto her daughter's hand.

The day of the big barbecue began on a sour note. Nado was abruptly woken by the sound of his mother's distressed voice. Mrs. Nell, driven by her instincts that something was wrong, had discovered that her baby girl had woken up earlier than both her and Nado and left the house once again. She didn't need to search the house or ask Nado about her whereabouts. Nado knew precisely why his mother was crying. Realizing that he must have been more exhausted than he initially thought, he sat on the bed, slowly shaking his lowered head from side to side.

"Well, it's about time you two woke up," said the voice at the door, startling Nado and Mrs. Nell as they looked up in surprise. Necy stood in the doorway, holding a tray of food she had prepared. She had woken up to find her brother's arm draped over her and her mother holding her hand. Her first thought was to escape their embrace, sneak out of the house, and find someone with drugs.

Carefully, she disentangled herself from her mother's grasp and delicately removed her brother's arm from her stomach. Once free, she quietly got off the bed, grabbed her purse, and headed for the door. As she eased it open, she glanced back at her sleeping mother and brother.

The scene reminded Necy of when they had slept together like this in the past – just the three of them against the world. Standing there made her realize something: Her mother could have given up on them after their father abandoned them, but she didn't. Her brother had recently been released from prison and could have been doing anything else aside from worrying about her, but there he was as well.

When she needed help, they were always there for her. Necy pushed the door open, placed her purse on the dresser, and walked to the kitchen. If she couldn't be strong for herself, how could she expect anyone else to be strong for her? Necy stood, looking at the confused faces of her mother and brother. "Well, don't just sit there. Come and help me."

Nado and Mrs. Nell sprang up and rushed toward Necy, accidentally causing a platter of food and juices to fall, crashing to the floor. In this house, breakfast was the least of their concerns. The only thing that truly mattered was ensuring that Necy was safe, secure, and taking her first real step towards truly coming home.

Lil Boot and JT Dollar, along with their hired help, set the grills ablaze. Music filled the air as people gradually gathered in the park. The promise of free food attracted all walks of life, and the crowd swelled in size. Almost everyone in town was either at the barbecue, on their way, or getting ready to join.

In short, the entire neighborhood was gearing up for a complimentary barbecue. However, not every attendee was primarily interested in the food. A specific group of individuals - the FBI - had been investigating ever since they'd heard about the event.

A free barbecue wasn't unusual, but what caught their attention was its grand scale. Announcements on the radio and ubiquitous flyers signaled significant expenses for someone – and nobody casually parted with that kind of money.

Local newspapers also monitored the event, setting up shop in anticipation. Both the FBI and news outlets were eager to uncover the underlying purpose behind this extraordinary gathering.

After the hugs and tears, Nado instructed everyone to get dressed for their busy day ahead. Mrs. Nell swiftly cleaned up the spilled food and donned the shirt Nado had given her. "Five minutes, everyone!" Nado called out as he dialed a number on the phone, waiting for the recipient to answer.

"Hello, this is Azurie. How may I help you?" "Hey there," replied Nado, "I just wanted to ensure you were awake." "Oh, I'm already dressed and waiting for you," Azurie said with a smile. She didn't mention that she'd been up all night in anticipation of the barbecue, repeatedly trying on and removing the shirt Nado had given her. "Are you on your way?" she asked.

"We'll be there in about 15 minutes. Are your parents still planning to attend?" In response, Azurie said, "I think they're looking forward to it even more than I am." "Well, I won't keep you. I need to hurry up my mom and Necy," Nado remarked.

"Necy? You found your sister?" Azurie inquired. Nado explained, "Well, not exactly. It was Dan who spotted and located me. He's getting a bonus for finding her." "Do you think he can manage all that money at once? It might not be much, but it's a lot for him," Azurie added.

"Don't you worry about old Dan? He can handle much more than that if only someone trusts him and gives him a chance. So, look out for us. We'll be coming by shortly," said Nado. After hanging up, he quickly called someone else and ushered his family into the car. "This will only take a minute," he told his mother and sister as he pulled into the motel parking lot. He approached room number 1 and knocked. The door opened automatically, and Nado stepped inside.

Nado had to take a second look at the man standing before him. Dressed in new clothes, clean-shaven, and sporting a fresh haircut, 2-4 looked like a completely different person.

"Well, I'll be damned. I wouldn't believe this if I weren't seeing it with my own eyes," said Nado as 2-4 stood back with a smile. He even wore a North Carolina Tar Heels cap.

"You look great, 2-4. How do you feel?" asked Nado. 2-4 walked away from Nado and stared at himself in the mirror. Nado waited patiently for him to answer the question.

"You know, I once looked like this heah. Dat wuz a long time ago," said 2-4. He smiled at Nado. "I thank I can git use to looking like dis again." With that, Nado felt relieved; he knew that before someone could better themselves, they had to start believing in themselves.

"Are you ready to work?" asked Nado. First, he reached into his pocket and pulled out a roll of bills. "Let me finish paying you for the first job I hired you for." Nado handed three one-hundred-dollar bills to 2-4. "You don't know how important what you did for me," said Nado.

2-4 stood next to Nado, counting the bills he had been given. "I have a special job for you today. My sister is in the car with me now. I don't want her to know you just yet, so you'll have to come to the park on your own. I want you to watch her for me. Stay back and act like you're there for the barbecue, but keep a close eye on her. If she leaves and you can't find me, use this phone to call me," said Nado.

Nado reached inside his coat, pulled out a bag with a phone inside, and handed it to 2-4. "All you have to do is open it up, press the on button, and it's ready to be used. By the way, try to be discreet about your identity," said Nado. "I've never seen a bag with a phone like this," commented 2-4. Nado replied, "This is new to me too, but we have to keep up with changing times. I'll see you when you get there."

2-4 looked at Nado with a puzzled expression. "The shirt," said Nado, "Change the shirt." Nado smiled as he turned to leave. "Oh, I almost forgot. Here's my personal number," Nado added.

When Nado arrived at the park, he was delighted by the turnout, particularly for that time of day. "I'll probably be busy all day, so enjoy yourselves, and I'll see you later," he told Mrs. Nell and Necy. Necy went to join Lil Boot and JT at the barbecue, while Nado took the opportunity to reassure his mother. "I know you're worried about Necy, but don't be. She'll be fine. Why don't you help with the refreshments?" Mrs. Nell hesitated but finally accepted his reassurance with a smile and walked away.

Azurie, who had been waiting for Nado's attention, stood before him, radiating beauty and strength. "I'm sorry I wasn't very chatty on the way over," he apologized. "Maybe you were embarrassed by your choice of date," replied Azurie playfully.

Taking her hand, Nado looked into her eyes and said firmly, "Choosing you for anything could never be a mistake. I could never be ashamed to be seen with you. There's a lot at stake today, and I wanted you here for a reason. I don't have to prove myself to anyone, but if I did, it would be you. Today is a huge step in my life, and I want you by my side. Wherever I am, there should you be, too. When people see me, they'll also see you."

Azurie was puzzled by Nado's words, but he tried to ease her confusion: "Just be patient a little longer, and everything will become clear soon enough. For now, let's go say hello to everyone."

It was now approaching 10 am, and the grass was barely visible on the ground. Music blared through the speakers as the crowd continued to grow. Nado navigated through the crowd, with Azurie clutching his arm tightly. Suddenly, he caught a scent that stopped him in his tracks, causing Azurie to bump into him. He scanned the nearby faces and was about to give up when he finally found the source. Without uttering a word, he dashed forward, tugging Azurie off balance. They stopped before a group of teenagers who were teasing one another. The teens briefly glanced at Nado before resuming their previous clowning.

"Give it to me," demanded Nado, capturing the group's attention. "I said, give it to me!" The young boy who had been smoking the joint tried to hide it by cuffing it in his hand and pulling his arm back. "What are you talking about? We're not doing anything," replied the teenager defiantly.

Nado approached the boy and pulled his arm from behind his back. "Not doing anything, huh? What is this, then? Either give me the rest of it now, or I'll take you to that police officer over there. Let's see what your parents think about you smoking marijuana." Nado waited for the group's decision.

"Just give it to him," one of the girls urged as she reached into her bra and retrieved a baggie full of marijuana. "Don't think we gave you that because you threatened us with our parents. They smoke more than we do. We just don't want any trouble with the law," explained one of the boys. The group turned and left while Nado shook his head at Azurie.

"If parents don't intervene with their children, we're in for a tough time," said Nado. He took Azurie by the hand and led her through the crowd. Along the way, they encountered several familiar faces Nado hadn't seen since his release from prison. They reached the platform where the DJ's equipment was set up and climbed the stairs. At the top, Nado paused to survey the larger-than-expected crowd, recognizing people he'd personally invited. He noticed Kong near the back, chatting with a group of young boys.

Nado didn't care about their conversation; what mattered was everyone's presence. This was his chance to define himself. Spotting a local news crew interviewing attendees, he thought that this event might surpass his expectations. Turning to Azurie, Nado said, "I've been planning this day for nearly a year. Today, you'll see and understand who I am now. You've played a significant role in my journey because if I hadn't met you, my life might be different. I'm going to put forth my will and ask Allah to touch the hearts of those who hear the sound of my voice." Confused, Azurie replied, "I don't understand what you're saying, Nado."

"Have you ever seen anyone spend over $30,000 to offer people free food, drinks, and entertainment? Nothing in life is free, Azurie and the price everyone will pay today is listening to what I have to say. I don't think the crowd will grow much more, so now seems like a good time," said Nado. Azurie gave Nado's hand an encouraging squeeze as he led her toward the microphone.

2-4 followed Necy everywhere she went, which hadn't been far. Smiling to himself, he thought of the easy money he was making. He watched as Necy set down her cup and began walking towards the back of the crowd. Assuming she was headed to the restroom, 2-4 trailed behind her. As expected, Necy entered the restroom and reemerged shortly after. The moment she stepped out, three men appeared from nowhere and grabbed her.

Necy struggled against them, but one of the men held what seemed like a towel over her face, causing her to collapse into the arms of another assailant. 2-4 were shocked by the sudden events and hesitated briefly. He saw Necy being dragged down a nearby trail but couldn't make his body move.

Thoughts of Nado and the bag phone finally snapped him out of his trance. 2-4 frantically dug into the bag to grab the phone. Once he retrieved it, he fumbled with the button in an attempt to turn it on. After finally pressing the button successfully, the screen lit up.

Frantically, 2-4 entered the digits Nado had given him. But just before pressing the last number, the phone died. He watched as three men dragged Necy further down the path, forcing him to make a decision. He could fight through the crowd and inform Nado, but if he did that, Necy would be gone. There was no doubt in his mind about what he had to do.

Without hesitation, 2-4 hurried towards the path where Necy was being taken. Perhaps he could catch up to them and thwart their intentions. He was determined to help Necy for Nado's sake, even if it took his last breath. After running 20 yards, 2-4 was nearly out of breath but driven by his desire not to let Nado down.

Suddenly, the music stopped. The only sounds were children playing nearby and muffled adult voices. The crowd's attention shifted to the platform where the DJ stood, but their gaze was on Nado. Standing at the edge of the platform, he held the microphone in one hand and raised the other to silence the crowd.

"As-Salaam-Alaikum," Nado began, "Most of you here today know me or have heard of me. 'This is it, BJ. Put the camera on the guy on the stage. I think we're about to find out what this day is all about," one of the agents said. Nado continued speaking, "For those who don't know me, my name is Alvernado Dexter. Everyone calls me Nado for short. What you are enjoying today has been provided by some of you yourselves. You may wonder how you could be responsible for this when you didn't donate a single cent. Although you haven't consciously contributed, your actions made all this possible. I was once involved in the drug trade and considered a major player. I've accepted money, TVs, VCRs, jewelry – anything valuable – in exchange for drugs. So, in a way, it is your money that I've used to provide what you're enjoying today."

Nado gave the crowd a moment to absorb his words. He couldn't tell by their facial expressions but was confident that he had struck a chord with some of them. He knew that even though not everyone used drugs, there was a chance they had a relative who did or had been burglarized by a drug addict seeking money to get high at some point in their lives.

Nado resumed his speech, "Let me emphasize this: nothing in life comes for free. For everything you receive, someone, somewhere, has made a sacrifice. Today, you must pay a price for the barbecue you're enjoying. That price is listening to me and my message. In the name of Allah, the Beneficent, the Merciful, I testify that there is no one to be worshipped but Allah, and Muhammad is His messenger. As I mentioned earlier, I was a drug dealer before discovering Islam. Now let me explain the essence of Islam – it's a faith that helps individuals understand their relationships with fellow humans and their Creator. I'm not here to preach; I simply wish to share some enlightening knowledge with you all.

At the very beginning, there existed only darkness. Would you concur? Visualize its hue - for those finding it difficult to understand my point, the color is black. Darkness equates to blackness. Thus, fundamentally, everything - living and non-living - emerged from this black abyss. Prior to the notion of Blackness, a divine entity existed, known as God or Allah. You may be familiar with the name Christopher Columbus, who is recognized in history as the discoverer of America in 1492. However, it is claimed that Indigenous People had already settled there. How can someone discover a place that's already inhabited? Allow me to take you on a short journey through history. Each nation has its unique language: The Chinese speak Chinese, the Japanese converse in Japanese, Russians communicate in Russian, and Africans use various native African languages, at least until the Europeans arrived. As the saying goes, "Birds of a feather flock together." Nations flourished without discord as long as they were undisturbed. However, Europeans, predominantly white men, observed the wealth of resources and affluence in the East and Africa. As a result, they schemed to exploit these territories.

The white man set foot in Africa and enticed the black man with prospects of prosperity and other allurements. But how could the white man fool the black man who was the possessor of divine wisdom? Was it not plausible that Africa could already cater to their lavish needs? The white man, capitalizing on the black man's compassionate nature, cunningly convinced him to embark on ships that steered him away from his homeland. With eloquent persuasion, the white man cleverly wheedled their leaders into endorsing his plans. And what more effective scheme to entice a black man than through another black man?

Ever since that day, the black man's life changed dramatically. On that fateful day, he was introduced to shackles and chains.

Why would someone supposedly going to a better place, aiming for self-improvement, be subjected to such restraints? It was the foundational lie among the countless others that would follow. That day marked the beginning of 400 years of unspeakable horror for a race of people destined for greatness. Though the oppressor was outnumbered, they possessed one distinct advantage over the original man - his humble nature. Whenever a black man disagreed with his captor, he would be tied up in plain sight, and the captor would order one of his so-called house niggas to beat the man unconscious as a lesson to others who watched.

The white man utilized the weapon of fear. When a Black man, fatigued from relentless mistreatment, would escape, the slave master would dispatch his faithful servants to hunt him down and return him, and then have one of them batter him to the brink of death. Everyone was force to watch this gruesome act. It's crucial to bear in mind that in America, the enslaved individuals were unfamiliar with the language, and the act of reading books was a transgression punishable by death. Thus, the question arises: who educated them about the United States? The answer is their very own slave master.

Do you think a person who seeks dominion over your every thought would take the trouble to impart even a modicum of their knowledge to you? After enduring 400 years of subjugation, the era arrived when it was no longer legally permissible for slave masters to claim ownership of a black man or woman. Hence, they convened and employed their power and influence to mold the Emancipation Proclamation to their liking. This decree supposedly bestowed freedom upon the enslaved individuals. But did it really? Following its ratification, these erstwhile slaveholders suddenly desired to present a Bible to their former captives - the very same individuals they had previously brutalized and occasionally murdered for daring to read any books over a span of 400 years. Why would a practice so deeply ingrained for four centuries be abandoned in a single day? I leave this for you to contemplate.

Sit the original man down and teach him how to read the Bible. How can a man who doesn't treat you right teach you properly? The first verses of the Bible taught to the original man by the slave masters were probably 'you shall not kill,' 'live by the sword, die by the sword,' and 'if you aren't good, you'll go to hell.' But the original man, with his humble nature, allowed himself to be kept in captivity. The slave master wasn't just targeting his strong body; he was out to capture his mind. 'God will take care of you. Just have faith.' Where was God when the Klan burned our ancestors' houses and left burning crosses in their yards? Do these teachings apply to the white man?

Do you know what a sword means in the Bible? It represents any weapon. The ropes our ancestors were hung with can be considered swords. Despite using their swords for 400 years, they now tell us it's wrong to use them. The Bible was given to the original man to instill fear and apprehension of divine retribution. Then, they granted the illusion of equality: allowing access to their front doors, water fountains, and education. However, they never permitted progress. Of course, they'll allow one or two individuals to climb the ladder of success, but with strings attached at every step."

Nado took a moment to survey the crowd, noticing that he had captivated everyone's attention. He caught a glimpse of Azurie smiling at him and felt reassured. Nado's gaze then fell upon Azurie's mother and father in the front row. He locked eyes with them briefly, and after receiving an approving nod and smile, Nado confidently continued his speech.

"It was orchestrated from the very beginning; the black man and black woman weren't meant to survive. The white man may have allowed us to drink from the same faucet he uses, enter through the same door, and eat from the same plates he does—but don't be fooled into thinking that he sees the black man as his equal. As for justice? For black men and women, this word holds a unique meaning: 'Just - us.' We must recognize that although the black race makes up only 13% of the United States population, we constitute 67% of those incarcerated across America. Who dominates the prison population in the United States? Let me hear you say it."

Nado held the microphone out towards the crowd as they answered, "Just us." He asked, "Is this what they meant by justice for all? The slave masters began making rules when they took our ancestors from Africa, and their descendants continue to make those rules today. Their false promises of 40 acres of land and a mule to plow never materialized for our ancestors after their liberation. The black man was freed not only in Harlem but across America. Can you imagine if the white man had kept his word? Maybe we would own this very park.

Yet, our black community must struggle continuously just to survive. We work hard every day to pay the slave master's rent for homes built on the land that should have been ours. While we may never receive those promised 40 acres or that mule, there is one thing we can reclaim: our pride. It is time for black men and women to stand up together and regain our pride.

Consider your offspring. Do you wish for them to face the same hardships you've endured? It doesn't need to be this way. We must impart knowledge to them about the harsh truths they might confront while they're still young. The slave master and his descendants have nothing to offer, particularly not to a black individual.

Cease perpetuating the falsehoods handed down by slave masters to our children. Take, for instance, the tale of Goldilocks and the Three Bears – the seemingly innocent white girl with golden hair who happens upon a house in the forest. She takes liberties with their home, trying out all the chairs, consuming their food, and testing all the beds before falling asleep in Baby Bear's bed.

The bears return to find their sanctuary invaded – their chairs sat in, their food eaten, and their baby's bed slept in. We need to alter such narratives because it's essential for our children to comprehend their identity without such skewed stories. In my neck of the woods, this behavior is termed as 'breaking and entering.'"

Though the crowd erupted in laughter, Nado gestured for silence. "I didn't share that to amuse you. I want you to grasp that it's time to equip our future generations with truth and wisdom, not the deceptions and folly that the slave master wishes us to instill in their bright young minds. Nowadays, children desire $200 Michael Jordan shoes or a shirt emblazoned with rapper Fifty Cent's image because we, as parents, fail to provide them with the role model they need at home. Picture a scenario where you're walking with your child, and their shirt reads 'The greatest.' Another kid comes over and inquires where they got that cool Michael Jordan shirt. Wouldn't you swell with pride to hear your child respond, 'This isn't a Michael Jordan shirt; this represents my mom or dad'? This can become a reality, but first, we need to enlighten ourselves and revert to the fundamental values our grandparents imparted to our parents. What is your mission in this life? I'm here today to declare to each one of you that Allah has a plan, and that plan won't alter to accommodate any individual's needs or wishes.

I'm certain each one of you has faced obstacles and will keep doing so until the day Allah decides to show mercy. Understand that finding your life's purpose is possible. Surrender to Allah and let Him guide you through both joyous and hard times. Remember, life's challenges are inevitable. Having Allah by your side can bring great solace. He will help you see through the deceptive words used by those who want to oppress you.

Not long ago, I had an engaging conversation with an elderly man who shared his nostalgic memories. He recalled that during the 1960s, a man just needed a large Afro to win a woman's heart. Then, from the mid-1960s to the early 1970s, stylishly leaning against a wall in clubs was the way to attract women; the one with the coolest demeanor would succeed. By the early 1980s, dancing became crucial, or else one might remain single. The wise gentleman observed that nowadays, young people have it easy as Afros, coolness, and dance moves aren't necessary.

Can you believe what he said? He claimed that with a nice car, money, and flashy possessions, anyone can attract any woman they desire. It's disheartening to see our brothers and sisters fall victim to the belief that material wealth is more important than self-respect. We live in a world where prejudice lurks beneath the surface; a world where wealth seeks more wealth and power craves more power, all while neglecting the poor."

Nado paused for a moment and surveyed the crowd. He still had their attention, but he was unsure how long it would last. Seizing the opportunity, he decided to share something thought-provoking. "May I tell you a little story?" he asked. Cheers erupted from the audience, with one person shouting, "Go ahead, brother, take your time." As a man started clapping, the rest soon followed suit. The atmosphere energized Nado. Glancing around, he noticed familiar faces – Lil Boot, JT Dollars, and his mother –

all smiling and clapping. Azurie's father also showed his support. Nado raised his hand, motioning for the crowd to calm down. Once they had settled, he continued, "During my extensive studies of Islam, I've encountered intriguing material and tales.

Today, I'd like to share an experience that a Black man had in the early 1940s. The emotions he experienced stemmed from the apparent murder of his father. His father had served in World War II, and it was reported that he had died during the war. However, the man later discovered that his father had been killed in Louisiana, a location not part of WWII. He found out that his father, a private, was shot during a peaceful protest led by black trainees at Camp Claiborne, Louisiana. The deadly shot was supposedly accidental, fired from an Army M-1 rifle. His father's protest had been impactful, angering white bigots at the camp and prompting black tankers to demand equal treatment. The man believed his father's death was no accident but a cold-blooded murder committed by those who had fought alongside him.

He became fixated on joining the military and eventually enrolled in the service. He transformed into a formidable soldier, earning the Silver Star for heroism. Tragically, his mother was killed by stray police bullets during a riot following Martin Luther King's assassination while she was in her top-floor apartment. This fueled his desire for retribution. He started by recruiting others like himself, including a black doctor. Together, they expanded their forces across different countries, uniting people of color from various regions. Their ultimate goal is to make the white man confront the truth about his actions. Remember that a doctor was part of this army. Their first operation involved using lasers to blind four white sheriffs. They executed it so effectively that all the sheriffs recalled was falling asleep and waking up sightless.

Next, he led his army to Detroit, taking down 60 drug lords. They displayed brutal acts on some of the defeated men, causing fear in the area. As a result, drug activities significantly decreased. He gained a reputation and was seen as a threat by many, from local criminals to law enforcement officers. Consequently, the FBI suspected him of conspiring against the government and wiretapped his phone, monitoring his conversations. This only heightened their conviction that he aimed to follow in the footsteps of Malcolm X or Martin Luther King. Allow me to read you his impassioned speech, which was recorded by the FBI.

"What do black men desire? Is it the same as everyone else, identical to the desires of white people? No, that's not enough. What we truly need, yearn for, and must have to find inner peace is Atonement. It's not about revenge or reparations for the injustices of the past, but rather Atonement. We all need to atone for our ancestors' decisions to board those slave ships, for believing in fanciful tales of abundant wealth in America. We must atone for allowing the heinous acts of white sailors and plantation overseers who violated black women and produced mixed-race children to be traded as commodities. Atonement is necessary for our political naivety and passivity during Reconstruction times.

For allowing those Klansmen to destroy our property and harm our loved ones, only to do it again. We should have united and defended ourselves against their violent acts. Instead, we sought solace in churches, singing hymns. We must atone for this. Take the Jewish community as an example - they know the importance of atonement. They transformed Israel into a nation of resilient fighters and equipped it with advanced weaponry. This is how they made amends for the millions who perished in Nazi gas chambers. That is true atonement.

That being said, the world should know that if Israel goes, so does the rest in a nuclear holocaust. However, some people still underestimate others, thinking they are unintelligent, lazy, and irresponsible. They believe that instead of working hard and improving ourselves, we only desire handouts – welfare, reverse quotas, or separate but equal treatment. These individuals fail to recognize that these offerings will never be enough because they don't comprehend the additional challenges each person faces. There's a need to prove not only one's worth but also the worth of an entire community.

Why don't they understand? They believe they've addressed the issue by providing us with religion, constantly feeding us their Christian beliefs since we were young enough to attend church. Martin, you claim you had a dream and saw the Promised Land? I argue that it was merely a dream. The church given to us by the white man and the notion of atonement have carried us as far as they can and as far as we need to go.

Now, we must face the consequences of our fall from grace, just like the devil. We have to learn to coexist in the same challenging environment. Don't accuse me of blasphemy or claim that violence isn't God's way. There are already enough people confined by their strong religious beliefs, which only serve as the oppressor's finest safeguard. Do you genuinely believe that all their singing and praying will persuade God to declare, 'Alright, children, I know I've neglected you and you've suffered hardships, but starting tomorrow, that will change. I'll ensure those in power love you and treat you like their equals'?

I've been to the mountain too, Martin, trying to follow you there. All I found were blind paths. I finally hit a way to the top. Oh, I know that I'm not gonna make it to the top alive, just like you didn't, but I got a glimpse of the peak. Einstein got a glimpse of something, too. Call it a unified wave theory.

Never saw it clear enough to prove. Only knew that proof was possible. What he tried to do with waves, I'm trying to do with people. All colored People."

Nado looked up before continuing. "There is more to this conversation, but I'm afraid that time will not allow me to finish it. If you would like to read more about what I have just spoken to you about, the book was written by *Marshall Goldburg, Intitled Critical List.* It's definitely an enlightening book.

Many of you here today have personally received an invitation from me to attend this gathering. Once, I was like you, but now I stand before you transformed. I shared that reading earlier to demonstrate that racism has existed long before our time and will continue to persist after we are gone. The man mentioned earlier sought atonement. Some of you might perceive him as evil due to his actions of blinding and killing others. Having read the entire book, I want to shed light on the real reasons behind his actions.

First and foremost, his father was killed by a government he had risked his life to protect. The reason he blinded those four sheriffs or government officials was to show them that not a single one of them was too powerful to be targeted. He also intended to instill fear in them. His missions were designed to create fear, and they succeeded. Next, he killed the drug lords. Why? Simply because they were poisoning the black community, destroying minds, and preventing them from reaching their full potential as the lions and tigers of the world. As a result, drug usage decreased significantly. Another mission accomplished. How many of you believe that he aimed to overthrow the government or instigate an all-out conflict with the authorities?

Nado noticed several hands raised in the crowd and smiled. "You're mistaken. That wasn't his objective. He desired an enlightened population to execute their right to vote. That's how he intended to combat racial injustices – through elections, just like everyone else. His goal was to increase Black representation in office, allowing the Black community more influence in the decisions that affected them. He recognized that empowering the Black psyche meant appealing to the Christian beliefs ingrained in them by white supremacy from the very beginning. But let's not assume that white supremacy is our sole adversary. As I mentioned earlier, they are cunning and very manipulative. White supremacy pits us against one another, handing us a Bible and preaching righteous behavior while threatening hell as punishment for disobedience.

Observe how they instilled fear in the black man. The ancestors of today's white man planted the idea of fire into the black man's mind centuries ago. They destroyed everything the black man tried to achieve and placed burning crosses in their yards. Each time they visited our ancestors, they left behind a lasting fear – fire. After programming the black man's mind to fear fire, they introduced the Holy Bible. They painted an alluring picture of heaven, a place of milk and honey, where streets are made of pure gold, and where you can reunite with loved ones if they lead virtuous lives on earth. Then, they reinforced that fear with the threat of fire.

CHAPTER TEN

Challenging Perceptions: The Struggle for Atonement and Empowerment

The Black man doesn't want to face hardship, so he must be good, humble, and endure anything the white man does to him just for a chance at prosperity, just for a taste of a better life. I'm here today to let you know that hell isn't beneath the earth. Hell is working for the white man, and after getting paid, going to another white man to borrow more money to combine with the little earnings you made just so you can afford some food to eat.

Hell is the constant worry for one's safety at home or while driving down the street. It's the fear of stopping at traffic lights due to the risk of carjacking. Hell is the daily uncertainty of job security. It's a life that we face each morning when we wake up. In today's world, we are surrounded by violence, theft, shootings, assaults, kidnappings, and child abductions. The internet is filled with websites promoting harmful content, making us question what awaits us after death.

Awaken, my cherished black brothers and sisters. Who has exhibited a violent nature throughout history? The white man. Conversely, the black man's nature is inherently good. We support and comfort each other in times of need. Consider this example: when your elderly parents require assistance, you adjust your life to accommodate theirs – it's the black man's nature. However, when white people face the same situation, they often send their parents to a nursing home for others to care for them. This behavior may stem from a self-centered and selfish mentality ingrained in their race that has even permeated high government offices.

Let's discuss drugs for a moment. Have you noticed the increasing variety of new drugs available today? Crack cocaine, ecstasy, crystal meth, and numerous others have emerged. It must have taken brilliant minds to create such substances. But who has the power, knowledge, and resources to invent these drugs and distribute them to the masses? We're not just talking about local distribution; we're talking about reaching an entire nation. Consider our government - the one that offers aid to foreign countries while millions of its own citizens go hungry. The same government that bombed part of Iran and supported other governments. Why does our government rush to help certain nations? It's important to recognize that it only aids those with valuable resources that we can use to better our country.

No resources, no help. Weapons of mass destruction - were the reasons our government gave for invading Iraq. They demanded that their president, Saddam Hussein, step down from his position of power. However, it is now known that there was no evidence of weapons of mass destruction. The true motive becomes clear: Iraq is a country rich in oil. Today, the nation is governed by individuals put in positions by our government. Perhaps Iraq should consider changing its name to "I-America."

Nado scanned the crowd, recognizing each face he had personally invited. "It's not just other countries that our government targets with its venom, but also the black community. The sophisticated drugs concocted by government scientists and the CIA were designed to devastate this community. They successfully infiltrated our streets with deadly poison. However, their plan wasn't foolproof. They failed to consider members of their own race who mingled with the black community. These individuals tasted the drugs, too, and became charmed by them. They turned on one of their white friends, and they turned on another until the white race was just as messed up on dope as the black race. What can we do now to correct our mistake?

They might be occupied at the moment, especially government scientists, working fervently to develop new solutions. Some of you might believe that crack was created by a black person since they are often seen selling it. However, they are being used as pawns by others. It is essential for us to unite against this exploitation and demand atonement. We're tired of seeing our community poisoned. Can you recall your parents or grandparents reminiscing about the good old days? Times when someone could receive a phone call from across town inviting them over without any concern. Or leaving their front door wide open and not worrying about returning home to find their belongings missing. Those truly were the good old days.

It is a proven fact that what goes around comes around, and I believe that together, you and I can make those times happen again. No, my friends, we have not endured the whips and chains that our ancestors went through, but in reality, we are still slaves—slaves of our own choosing. Education is the key to breaking free from the chains of bondage that bind the people of this world today. We may not be able to save the entire world, but we can make a difference in our community.

We cannot control drugs once they enter our bodies. Don't you understand that drugs are designed to destroy our spirit, particularly that of the black community? The use of these substances directly impacts our ability to thrive and reproduce. My fellow brothers, I appeal to you today – stand up and embody the role you were meant to play as kings of the land. Show our beautiful black sisters that they can avoid the objectification and lustful gaze of those who seek to control them. If you continue using these harmful substances, it only serves their goals and perpetuates a cycle of elimination through incarceration or addiction-fueled violence.

Black men, before you can uplift the black women in your life, focus on empowering yourself first. And to all the strong black sisters out there, stand your ground and embrace your identity as queens. Do not allow anyone to treat you with anything less than the respect you deserve. You are a beautiful creation that should be treasured and protected. Do not let harmful influences take control of your lives or relationships. If your partner refuses to stop using drugs, consider seeking a relationship with someone who truly values and respects themselves and those around them – a true king rather than a pawn who perpetuates harmful cycles. We must train our bodies to effectively combat the devil and his devious tactics."

The crowd erupted in applause as Nado scanned the audience. Despite searching intently, he couldn't spot the person he was looking for. Perhaps they had other commitments. Regardless, his message would reach Kong through the barbecue. 2-4 spotted the three men as they disappeared off the main trail, dragging Necy's lifeless body behind them. Cautiously, 2-4 approached the path and, finding it clear, ran as fast as he could in an attempt to catch up to the men escaping with Necy.

As he ran, he thought about Nado. He had to rescue Necy. Nado had placed immense trust in him, and there was no way he was going to let him down. 2-4 pushed himself harder along the path, and just as he approached its end, he came face to face with three men standing over the lifeless body of Necy.

"Get your nosy ass out of here before you get into something you can't handle, old man," said one of the boys. 2-4 replied, "What are you doing to that woman on the ground? I think yawl best let her be and go on bout yawl business." The guys' attention shifted to something happening in the street. 2-4 was no longer their primary concern as they watched the gold Mercedes turn the corner. "I said leave the woman alone," repeated 2-4. As 2-4 started walking towards the group, he regained their attention.

"I told you, you old fool, to mind your business, didn't I? I'm giving you one more chance to go on and mind your own business," the young man said. 2-4 acted as though he hadn't heard him speaking. He continued walking, ready to sacrifice himself if necessary. Exhausted from the long run he had just completed, 2-4 barely managed a swing as the group of young men charged at him. It was practically over the moment one of the guys landed a blow below his ribs, knocking the remaining wind out of his body that he had lost from the run.

The only thing that 2-4 could do was cover his head with his arms and hope that the assailants would leave Necy alone and unharmed. The attackers made 2-4 suffer as they struck his body from all directions. A swift kick landed in his groin, causing him to lose grip of one hand in an effort to shield his face. This action left him vulnerable, allowing for a forceful kick to land squarely on 2-4's face, causing blood to pour from his nose. 2-4 had thought the assault would have ceased by now, but it only intensified. Just as he felt himself on the verge of passing out, a car horn blasted through the air. As suddenly as it had started, the aggression ended. The individual responsible for sounding that horn had most likely saved 2-4's life.

He felt himself being dragged along the ground, wondering what these attackers had in store for him. The thought of them assaulting a woman was horrifying enough, let alone an elderly man like himself. Determination surged through him as he prepared to gather the last of his strength for another attempt to fend them off. Suddenly, his body ceased moving. Cautiously, he opened his eyes and was astonished to find no one there. His thoughts shifted to Necy, and with a surge of energy, he managed to rise onto his knees and look in the direction where he had seen her lying earlier. She had left, and so had the three men.

2-4 struggled to his feet and stumbled towards the end of the path. He arrived just in time to see Necy being pushed into the back seat of a large, pretty gold car – the one he saw daily near the coffee shop while scavenging in the dumpster. As 2-4 staggered towards the car, the men closed the back door, and he felt that he had let Nado down. Falling to his knees helplessly, he watched the impressive gold vehicle speed away from the curb. "Gotta git to Nado, gotta git to Nado," 2-4 whispered to himself as he slowly crawled back towards the path he had just left.

Kong smiled to himself as he drove through the deserted streets. "I knew it was only a matter of time before I caught up to you, Baby Boo," said Kong. He found himself waiting at a traffic light, eager for it to turn green. Glancing at the car next to him, Kong was met with a puzzled expression. The elderly woman quickly averted her gaze and stared straight ahead, wishing for the light to change. At first, she assumed the man was talking to himself, but then she considered how she, too, sometimes listened to the radio and sang out loud.

The light finally turned green, and Kong waited for the old lady to drive away. She had unnerved him, as he thought she had seen the men forcing Baby Boo into the back seat of his car. Before leaving, Kong glanced across the seat and found Baby Boo staring at him wide-eyed.

"Well, well, well. Why did you run out on me like that, Baby Boo? You know I'm a very busy man. I said I'd be back as soon as I could. I even had something for you—something you like. In fact, it's still at the house. What do you say about going over to my place and hanging out?" Kong spoke to Necy as though he had everything under control. If he had known she was awake while he stopped at the traffic light, he might have panicked, jumped out of the car, and forcibly placed her in the front seat beside him to prevent her from attempting to escape. Fortunately, everything seemed alright now.

"What happened to me? I remember someone grabbing me, and then everything went black. How did I get in your car?" asked Necy. Kong saw his opportunity and seized it. The one thing he prided himself on was his ability to talk. "I was using the restroom when I came out and saw three guys attacking a woman. I had no idea it was you at the time. When I realized I did what I had to do. By then, you were unconscious, so I carried you to my car. Fortunately, I was parked nearby. The rest is history."

Kong offered Necy a reassuring smile as he continued driving toward his house. Sitting up in the back seat, Necy glanced into the rear-view mirror, catching Kong's gaze. "Thank you so much for helping me. I don't even want to imagine what would have happened if you hadn't been there," Necy said, her childlike grin warming Kong's heart. She leaned back in her seat and closed her eyes, feeling a mixture of relief and annoyance at the events that had transpired. The memory played vividly in her mind – emerging from the restroom only to be accosted by three men. She'd tried to fend them off but soon realized it would be useless.

She was about to scream when one of the men placed a cloth over her face. Instinctively, she held her breath and went limp after a few seconds. Once the cloth was removed, she resumed breathing. As they led her along the path, she discreetly peeked to see where they were headed. When they laid the cloth on the ground, they didn't touch her again. Someone had attempted to help her, but his identity remained a mystery. That person had paid a hefty price for trying to assist her. Hearing the sound of a car horn and seeing the vehicle made her understand what was happening. Now, she had to play along with this twisted game. He must have known that his money was gone; why else would he have abducted her from the park? Necy opened her eyes as the car came to a halt.

"We're here, Baby Boo. Come on, let's go inside, and I'll get you something to drink," said Kong. He got out of the car and opened the back door for Necy. As they walked towards the house, Kong waved and smiled at his neighbor who was outside watering his lawn. He opened the door, and just as Necy was about to enter the house, Kong gave her a forceful shove, causing her to fall onto the floor. "Game over for you – little bitch. Where the fuck is my money?" demanded Kong. Necy lay motionless on the floor, looking up into the angry face of Kong.

As Nado prepared to conclude his speech, he noticed a commotion stirring in the crowd. It wasn't the kind that would occur during a fight, so he ignored it and continued speaking. Moments later, Azurie's scream caught his attention. Nado glanced back and followed her gaze toward the stairs. Dropping the microphone, he rushed towards 2-4, who mustered his last ounce of strength to crawl to Nado before collapsing. Nado knelt beside 2-4, lifted his head, and placed it in his lap. The crowd fell silent, watching in shock.

"Gone," 2-4 barely whispered. "Tried to stop." Confused, Nado asked, "Gone? What do you mean by 'gone,' 2-4?" Bloodied and beaten, 2-4 struggled to explain. Azurie approached and recognized him despite his injuries. "Nado, is that Dan? You keep calling him 2-4." Hearing Azurie's voice prompted 2-4 to open his eyes and offer her a sad smile. "It's me, Zurie. I tried to protect her, but they took her anyway," he said weakly while gripping Nado's shirt. "I didn't mean to let you down—I tried real hard." Tears welled up in 2-4's eyes as Azurie took his hand tenderly in hers.

"Oh, Dan, what happened to you?" Azurie asked. "Dey attacked Necy when she left the bathroom. I tried to fight them, but they were young and strong," 2-4 replied. Hearing his sister's name, Nado grew firm. "Who attacked her? Tell me who did it and where she is!" Nado demanded. 2-4 took a moment to collect himself, wincing from the pain inflicted by the young men. He attempted to offer a weak smile to Nado and Azurie, but the agony prevented him from doing so.

"Never seen dem afore. Dey put her in a car - the same car dat be at the lil coffee shop. You've seen it afore. I saw you ridin in it afore," said 2-4. Nado was confused, as he couldn't recall any car from the coffee shop that he had ridden in. "I've only ridden in my own car and my partners' cars." He glanced at his partners, who were staring intently at him. Nado continued, "It can't be their car because they're here." 2-4's next words stopped Nado in his tracks. "The big, flashy gold car always be parked at the coffee shop - Dat's the car I seen dem guys put hur in." Nado swiftly grabbed Azurie by the arm.

"I have to go get my sister. Take care of him for me; my mother will help you," said Nado. He jumped up and rushed down the stairs and through the crowd. Like clockwork, Lil Boot and JT followed closely behind. The onlookers stared in stunned silence.

"Don't just stand there, BJ. Pack up the equipment, and let's go. I have a feeling that something major is about to happen," said one of the female reporters. She wasn't the only one with that intuition. The FBI agents were on their walkie-talkies, assembling their team and directing them toward the direction in which Nado and his associates had fled.

Before she could respond to Kong's question, she suddenly found herself on the receiving end of a backhanded slap. She fell face-first onto the floor and began to scream. Never before had she encountered such a situation in her life, not even recalling a childhood spanking. Instinctively, her mind urged her to roll away, and she did so just in time, as Kong's foot landed where her head had been moments prior. If he wanted a fight, then a fight is what he would get.

Necy, surprisingly skillful at this, raced for a lamp as Kong charged toward her. As he reached out to grab her, she nimbly ducked under his arm—much like she had done with the wino in the alley— and sprinted for the fireplace. When Kong regained his balance and turned around, he found himself facing Necy's menacing grin as she stood with a fire poker raised high above her head. "Come on, if you want me that bad," Necy screamed. Observing her trembling hands holding the poker aloft, Kong knew he had to think quickly. He raised his hands in a gesture of surrender.

"Let's discuss this calmly, Baby Boo. It doesn't need to be this way. I simply got carried away. I'm not accustomed to having anyone steal from me. I usually deal with little thug-ass troublemakers when they step out of line. Please put the poker down, and let's talk this through," said Kong. Necy stood trembling with tears streaming down her face. He had deceived her once; why should she trust him now? "Wait, I want to make a peace offering," said Kong.

Cautiously, he stepped back until he reached the kitchen counter. He slowly opened the small sliding drawer and reached in. Pulling his hand out, he lifted the plastic bag and held it out for Necy to see clearly. He watched her reaction, and upon seeing it, a smile emerged on his face. "I won't hurt you again. I already apologized for what I did, and I understand that if I had acted differently, you wouldn't have taken my money. Put the poker down, and let's relax in the den," said Kong.

Necy knew Kong wasn't being truthful. She was aware that had she not obtained the poker, she might be in a bloody state now. But above all else, she hoped to enjoy what Kong held in his hand before anything else happened. Necy lowered her head and gently placed the poker on the floor. Cautiously, Kong approached her, took the poker from her hand, and gently guided her by the elbow towards the den. The only sounds Necy heard were the poker hitting the floor and the rustling of the bag in Kong's hand as it brushed against her arm with each step they took.

"Head to the little coffee shop," Nado shouted to Lil Boot as they pulled out of the park's parking lot. "What's going on, Nado? Who was that man that crawled up on stage?" asked Lil Boot. "Kong... Kong sent guys to kidnap Necy from the park. The guy on stage was 2-4," replied Nado. "Who the heck is 2-4, and why would Kong kidnap Necy from the park?" asked JT.

"Do you remember when we went to McDonald's, and I talked to that old man in the parking lot? That was 2-4. I had him watching Necy at the barbecue," said Nado. "He told me she went to the restroom, and when she came out, they attacked her. He tried to stop them but got beaten up instead. He saw them put Necy into Kong's car."

"I knew we should've dealt with that low-life son of a bitch when we had the chance," said JT Dollar. "What I don't understand," said Nado, "is why would Kong kidnap Necy in the first place." JT snapped, "Honestly, it doesn't matter why he did it now. He crossed the line, and his ass will be dealt with."

Lil Boot drove Nado's BMW through the city streets, pushing the speedometer well past its limits. They even passed a police car, which seemed to fade away into the distance. Whether the police were just eager to clock out or had bigger fish to fry, Lil Boot couldn't tell. Regardless, he was grateful for the apparent distraction from their mounting troubles.

"Copy that. Subjects just passed me, and they seemed to be in a big hurry. Are you sure you don't want me to pursue?" asked the officer. "Negative. Fall back and let us handle the situation, copy?" replied the FBI agent. "10-4, over and out," said the officer.

Whatever was about to happen, the feds didn't want anything to interfere, so they contacted city police and briefed them on the situation. Lil Boot thought that luck was on his side, but it wasn't luck at all - simply meticulous caution. As the feds followed the black BMW from a distance, they suddenly noticed unexpected company. Unaware that the feds were also tailing them, BJ unknowingly sped past the pursuing federal car in the news van while Cindy clung to the dashboard, pointing and shouting directions.

"What on earth?" One of the federal agents exclaimed. The agent in the passenger seat turned just in time to see the news van whizz past them. His partner, who was driving, glanced into the rearview mirror and noticed the van swiftly approaching. It wasn't until the van pulled up alongside them that he fully understood what was happening. "I should've known they'd follow us. There's not much we can do without giving ourselves away," the agents grumbled.

"Perhaps we can try something that won't attract the BMW occupants' attention." The driver of the agent's car pressed down on the accelerator. Gradually, their car gained ground until it was parallel with the news van. BJ looked to his left and saw a man holding a badge against the car window.

"We've got company, Cindy," said BJ, watching as the man rolled down his window and motioned for him to do the same. "We can't lose them. Act like you don't see them and keep going." Cindy was an aggressive reporter who had gone to great lengths to get her stories, but she had mostly been on her own during those times. "I know your reputation, Cindy, and I respect your aggressive approach to getting your stories. But I just landed this job, and I like it," BJ added, slowly rolling down his window.

"FBI!" the man shouted at BJ, "If you continue to pursue that car, you could be interfering with a federal investigation. We'd like you to pull your van in behind us, and if you choose to follow, that's your choice." The agent spoke firmly. BJ glanced at Cindy, who nodded her approval. He gave the man a thumbs-up and watched as the federal agents sped off.

"I knew something big was going on; the Feds don't get involved unless it's significant," BJ said. Cindy quickly noted down details as they followed the agents' car at a safe distance.

Azurie's father had helped 2-4 off stage after his ordeal, taking him to the emergency room for treatment before releasing him. They now sat at Nado's house drinking coffee while 2-4 discussed his experience.

Although 2-4 had suffered a broken nose and bruised ribs during the attack, doctors assured him he would recover quickly. He noticed Mrs. Nell staring intensely at him – her gaze so fierce that he found himself focusing on other things. As he examined the pictures on the wall, they seemed compelling enough to draw him out of his seat.

Azurie and her father were observed in a confused state of understanding as 2-4 moved from picture to picture, looking at each of them with a sad expression on his face.

"Are you ready to leave, Mr. Dan?" asked Mrs. Nell. Her sudden outburst startled Azurie and surprised her father. Azurie stared at Mrs. Nell, thinking her comment was rude and inappropriate. She wondered if Mrs. Nell assumed that just because Dan was homeless, he would steal from her home. Azurie decided that if Dan wasn't welcome, she didn't want to be there either.

"Father, are you ready to go?" Azurie's father acknowledged her and told Mrs. Nell it had been a pleasure meeting her. Azurie watched as Dan took one last look at the pictures on the wall before turning to Mrs. Nell. "I did the best I could. Please take good care of dem kids," said Dan, lowering his head as he walked through the door.

No one said much as they rode through the busy streets. Azurie glanced at Dan and felt the urge to lift his spirits. "What about that lunch you offered to buy me the other day? Is the offer still valid?" Azurie waited for a response, but Dan remained lost in his thoughts.

"Dan, did you hear me?" asked Azurie, prompting him to snap out of his trance and face her. "I'm sorry, Zurie. I was just thinking about things—what ifs and all that. You know, doing the right thing the first time can sho save a person a lot of heartache. I think I need some rest," said Dan, turning to stare out of the window.

Azurie's father's voice brought him back to reality: "Here we are, Mr. Dan. If there's anything I can do for you, let Azurie know." Dan opened the door and stepped out of the car with Azurie by his side immediately afterward.

"Dan, are you alright? Did Mrs. Nell say something upsetting? You know I worry about you," said Azurie. Dan smiled at Azurie and placed his hand on her shoulder. "Mrs. Nell shouldn't hold anything against you. She can see by the beating you took that you did what you could to stop them," Azurie added. "I'll be fine. I just need to git a little rest, that's all," Dan reassured her. He noticed the way Azurie was looking at him. "Why are you looking at me like that?" Dan asked.

"You look so different than before, almost younger. If you don't mind me asking, how old are you?" inquired Azurie. Dan looked at Azurie and smiled. "I guess that wuz a compliment, and I appreciate it. I'm only 42 years old. All that hair made me look at least 20 years older, didn't it?" Dan responded.

"It certainly made a difference," said Azurie. She glanced at her father, noticing his growing impatience. "Well, I should get going. Are you sure you'll be alright?" she asked.

"I'm sure I'll be just fine. Thanks for everything," replied Dan. Azurie handed him a piece of paper. "Here's my number if you need to talk or anything," she said. With that, Azurie walked to the car where her father waited. Dan watched until the car disappeared from view before entering the room.

He didn't turn on the television or the radio. Instead, he sat on the empty bed and began to reminisce. He thought about his childhood and how his parents had provided everything they could to give him a chance in life. He had done well, even marrying at one point. However, his life grew confusing, and he struggled to cope with its challenges and responsibilities.

In his confusion, Dan had abruptly left his struggling wife and their two children behind. He moved to another state and continued living a life that only added to his confusion. Eventually, he returned to his hometown, but few people recognized him beneath the filthy clothes and long hair that covered his head and face.

He would often stand back and observe a particular woman as she carried out her daily activities. Once, their eyes met, and for the briefest moment, he saw a flicker of recognition in her gaze before she turned and ran away. Later on, he felt a watchful presence while rummaging through dumpsters or collecting cans. When he looked up, he would spot the woman at a distance, silently observing him.

Just as abruptly as she began watching him, she stopped. His suspicions were confirmed – she had known his identity for the past three years but never approached him. If only he could have been the man he was striving to become now. 2-4 sat in the quiet room, contemplating the possibilities.

"Hey man, where did you learn to talk like that? I've never heard you speak in that way before. Is that what you were doing while you were away? That shit was really deep. I've never just sat back and considered things the way you explained them today. I'm telling you, man, everyone could feel it." Lil Boot said. Nado was only half listening to Lil Boot as he spoke. His mind and attention were focused on something just around the corner. As Lil Boot turned the corner, Nado had risen completely out of his seat, anticipating Kong's car parked at the little coffee shop. He slumped back in his seat after seeing that only two cars occupied the lot, neither of which belonged to Kong.

"Pull into the lot," Nado said. Before the car came to a complete stop, Nado jumped out and sprinted toward the door. Red Ball saw Nado approaching and could tell by his expression that something urgent was happening. Nado ran straight to the counter and locked eyes with Red Ball.

"Where is Kong? I don't have time for games, so if he's here, just tell me," Nado demanded. "He isn't here. I haven't seen him since early this morning. He mentioned going to a barbecue." Nado trusted Red Ball's honesty; after all, he had witnessed JT

Dollar and Lil Boot's actions. Time was of the essence, so Nado dashed back to the car.

"Let's go, he's not here. There's only one other place he could be," Nado said. Lil Boot sped out of the parking lot without needing further direction. As they zoomed past the FBI car and news van parked around the corner, all eyes were on them. "Attention all cars: subjects are on the move again, heading north on Parks Blvd. Maintain a safe distance from them," an agent radioed in. The feds allowed the black BMW to drive about a block and a half before following suit.

"They're still following us," said the driver of the federal car. The agent in the passenger seat responded, "Well, they must sense that something big is about to happen. They have a knack for that kind of thing. I'm just surprised they haven't updated us on the identity of the bloody man who crawled onto the stage. You know how those state guys can be. Maybe we should've left one of our own agents; we'd probably know what's going on by now."

The other agent replied, "Why don't you call the Lieutenant again and see if he has any new information? If he doesn't, ask him to make some calls and find out what the state agents have discovered."

The driver responded, "You make the call; I need to focus on driving." The agent in the passenger's seat took out his phone and began dialing.

Cindy, in the news van, told BJ, "Don't lose sight of them. This could be your big break." BJ grinned as he trailed the FBI car. "That's exactly what I need," Cindy agreed.

Meanwhile, at the Dexter's' house, Mrs. Nell sat at the kitchen table, staring into her cup of coffee. She had always kept her secret close to her heart. Life had treated her well until she saw a ghost one day. She hadn't believed in ghosts before, but that changed three years prior. The sighting shocked and frightened her so badly that she ran away. However, she couldn't accept that it was a ghost and found herself drawn to the spot where it appeared.

At first, when she sought out the ghost, it didn't show up. But she persevered, and eventually, the ghost reappeared without scaring her anymore. She had always shared her experiences with her children, but this secret remained hers alone. She couldn't bring herself to tell them about the ghostly encounter. The last time she saw it, it was just inches away – close enough to touch – but she never intended to reach out or see the ghost again. Numerous times, she wished it had never appeared to her at all. Now, she wondered if others could see the same apparition and if it looked the same to them. Night after night, she prayed that this ability wasn't hereditary; she definitely didn't want Nado and Necy to see this ghost.

———

CHAPTER ELEVEN

A Mother's Silent Struggle: Unraveling the Past, Embracing the Present

Exhausted, Mrs. Nell realized she needed sleep after a long day. She rose from her seat, leaving the cup of coffee untouched on the table, and headed to her room. Lying down on the bed, she thought about Nado and how her prayers had been answered. She was uncertain about the identity of Allah, whom her son mentioned, but she knew that He had given Nado a new purpose in life. As Mrs. Nell drifted off to sleep, thoughts of Nado's speech filled her mind; however, the image of the ghost occasionally invaded her thoughts.

"There it is," said Nado, spotting the gold Mercedes as they turned the corner leading to Kong's house. "How should we handle this?" asked JT Dollar. Lil Boot stared at him. "There's only one way to handle it: kick in the door and deal with his ass," Lil Boot replied. Nado was trying hard to change his ways, but a person can only be pushed so far. JT Dollar waited for Nado's response, but none came.

"Stop right here," instructed Nado. They sat in silence, studying the layout of the house. The windows were secured with burglar bars, eliminating that option for entry. Nado knew what had to be done and turned to Lil Boot. "It's up to you to get us inside the house. Can you, do it?" asked Nado. Lil Boot looked toward the home, understanding what Nado was referring to. He had done it several times in recent years and had become quite proficient at it.

"Let's do this," said Lil Boot. Nado and JT opened their doors and, as quietly as possible, let them close behind them. It took Lil Boot a little longer to get his door open. Not because there was something wrong with it, but just like a visa, he never went to work without it. He leaned over and slid his hand under the seat where he had been sitting, pulling out his chrome-plated .357. He tucked it into his pants, covered it with his shirt, and finally opened his door to join his partners on the other side of the car.

"Be careful," warned Nado. "My baby sister is inside that house." Without hesitation, Nado and his companions crouched down and slowly inched their way toward Kong's front door, using bushes and trees as cover.

"It's happening. Subjects are out of their car and attempting to sneak up on the green house the second dwelling from the end of the street. Everyone, get into position and wait for my signal before moving in," instructed the FBI agent. Simultaneously, someone else was issuing their own orders.

"Move it, BJ!" shouted Cindy. "Capture the whole scene. Zoom in on every detail. Get shots of those agents closing in on the house." BJ enthusiastically worked his camera, zooming from one point to another. This was why he had entered this field.

Grinning, he focused his camera on the three men cautiously approaching the front of the large greenhouse.

Necy didn't need any more drugs, as she was already incredibly high. Nevertheless, she continued to smoke the large pieces of crack that Kong provided on the glass pipe. Suddenly, Necy stood up and slowly walked toward the window. Kong observed her with amusement; he knew exactly what was going through her mind since he had seen this scenario play out many times before with other addicts. He anticipated her comments about the police or someone being outside.

Kong had grown accustomed to this behavior. As Necy approached the window, he reminisced about a time when he took two women to a motel room during a harsh storm. The lightning illuminated the sky every time it struck. One woman enjoyed intimacy under the influence, while the other, like Necy, constantly peered out of the window. Kong and one woman engaged in their activity while lightning flashed outside. Startled, the other girl withdrew from the window and pulled her friend away, exclaiming that someone had taken her photograph.

Kong could laugh about it now, but at that moment, he hadn't realized crack caused hallucinations for some people. He understood this now and wasn't surprised by anyone's actions anymore. That's why he kept providing Necy with large amounts of crack cocaine; he wanted to exploit every opportunity to cause pain in their lives indirectly through Baby Boo's suffering. He had accepted his own downfall by involving them in his troubles and looked at Baby Boo as she peeked out of the window. Kong smiled again, knowing that pain comes in various ways. He sat back and observed as Necy began to waver.

Necy's eyes darted from side to side, scanning the entire yard. She was certain she had just seen a white man in a suit duck behind the house next door. Perhaps she was only imagining things, like she used to when she and Boss Player got high. She would be convinced that someone was watching them from outside. Recalling how she flushed Pretty Tony's stash down the toilet, thinking the police were about to raid their home. But each time they had taken her outside, no one was there. Maybe she was imagining things again.

Her thoughts were suddenly interrupted by what seemed like movement once more; this time, it came from the back of the house she was in. A white face emerged from behind the large tree, and for a second or two, she remained frozen.

Necy released the curtain and stepped away from the window. Her face filled with horror, she turned to Kong, "They're out there. I saw them, Kong. They're out there." Kong stood and walked over to the bookcase lining the wall. He crouched near its center and pressed down on the carpet with his thumb, revealing a hidden safe behind the shifting bookcase. Kong dialed the combination and opened the safe, exposing piles upon piles of cocaine in both powder and rock form.

He reached in, grabbed a bag containing crack rocks, and scooped a handful. As he removed his hand, several rocks fell to the floor. He turned to Baby Boo, who still wore her terrified expression.

"I told you I had something for you," said Kong. "Quit worrying about what's outside and enjoy yourself." Necy grew hysterical at the sight of so much dope and yelled at Kong, "I told you they're out there! I saw them, Kong! They'll be here any second!" Remaining calm, Kong approached Necy and took her by the hand.

"Let me worry about them, Baby Boo. Just enjoy yourself. Let's go to the bedroom and have some fun. Maybe I can find something to help you forget about the people outside." Kong gently pulled Necy towards the bedroom, but she broke free and hurried back to the window. Peering through the curtain, she saw only the stillness of the yard, disturbed only by a bird startled from the windowsill by her sudden movement. Kong approached her and touched her shoulder softly.

"You're safe with me, Baby Boo," said Kong. "As long as you're with me, nothing will happen to you." Necy considered that maybe she was just imagining things, as she had done many times before. She accepted the pipe from Kong and ignited the massive rock atop it. As she exhaled the smoke, her mouth remained open in surrender. Dazed and oblivious, Kong led Necy to their final destination: his bedroom.

Lil Boot stood at the door, his adrenaline surging out of control. He glanced at JT, who nodded in approval, then at Nado, who held up a finger. Nado brushed past Lil Boot and reached for the door handle, whispering a plea to himself as he started to turn it slowly. Preparing to relinquish control to Lil Boot once more, Nado knew he was only delaying what had to be done - but he couldn't stop turning the knob until it slowly creaked open.

Nado opened the door just enough to see inside the house. Satisfied, he signaled his partners to follow him. The three of them quietly slipped into Kong's house.

"All units move in, I repeat, move in." Federal agents emerged from various hiding spots, such as behind trees and neighboring houses. They converged on the green house with precise execution.

Nado and his partners stood silently, listening for any sounds that would reveal Kong and Necy's location within the house. The silence was suddenly broken by music coming from a room down the hall. Nado and his partners quickly closed in on the source of the music. There, Nado heard Kong's unmistakable voice.

"I think we have some unfinished business," said Kong. Nado heard what sounded like a slap, followed by his sister Necy screaming hysterically. That was all the motivation Nado needed to burst through the door. The room he entered was large and cluttered with various types of furniture. It wasn't long before he heard Kong's startled voice.

"What the hell?" exclaimed Kong. Quickly realizing what was happening, he reacted swiftly. He had been naked, planning to have rough sex with Necy, but those plans were now on hold as he lunged for the bed. Nado saw what Kong was attempting to do but couldn't act fast enough to stop him.

The sight of his naked sister standing next to the bed, holding her face, momentarily froze him. He realized the situation but wasn't as quick as Kong. By the time Nado had made it halfway across the room, he found himself staring down the barrel of a small-caliber pistol.

"So, you came to save the crackhead, did you?" said Kong. He had been terrified when Nado and his partners barged into the room but, as usual, regained control of everything. "You fools dare invade my territory? Who's going to save you now?" asked Kong.

Lil Boot trailed behind Nado but couldn't hide completely from Kong. If he reached for his gun, Kong would have the upper hand. He had to be patient. In a split second, Kong unexpectedly raised his pistol towards Necy's head.

Kong noticed Nado inching closer and instantly aimed the pistol at him. Realizing the danger, Necy looked at Kong, her mind going blank. Her only thought was to prevent Kong from shooting her brother. She lunged at Kong, who reacted like an experienced street veteran.

He fired his pistol point-blank into Necy, but her momentum carried her forward. The impact knocked the gun from Kong's hand as she collided with him. This was the opening Lil Boot needed. He grabbed his gun from his waistline and stormed across the room, smashing it into Kong's face.

Nado and JT's attention turned to Necy, who lay motionless on the floor. Both rushed and knelt down beside her. Nado whispered reassuringly in her ear, "Come on, Necy baby, everything is going to be alright." Just as he instructed JT to call an ambulance, the clamor of shouting voices froze him in place.

"Freeze!" shouted the FBI agents. "Put the gun down and place your hands on top of your head." Nado understood the command clearly but was puzzled as to why they were telling him to drop the gun. It was Kong who had held the weapon, which Necy had knocked out of his hand. Was Kong armed again? In the chaos of seeing his sister fall, he had lost track of Kong.

"I said put the gun down now," reiterated the agents. Following their gaze, Nado spotted something shocking: Lil Boot was sitting on Kong's chest, mercilessly pummeling his face with the large pistol. Blood gushed from Kong's head and splattered Lil Boot's shirt and arms.

While everyone was focused on Lil Boot's relentless assault, Necy began to stir. "Don't make me do it," shouted an officer, but Lil Boot continued pounding the pistol against Kong's skull.

"Lil Boot," uttered Necy's weak but unmistakable voice. "Please stop, Lil Boot." Awakened from his violent trance by her plea, he realized a dozen officers had surrounded him with guns drawn. Oblivious to their presence, he had been fixated on avenging Necy and defending himself from an assumed threat. He carefully lowered the gun and crouched beside Kong's head.

"Put the gun down and place your hands on your head," commanded an officer. Glancing at Kong, a flash of what he'd tried to do to Necy surged through Lil Boot's mind. His grip on the pistol tightened as he noticed Kong's neck pulsating amidst a pool of blood. Wavering, he began lifting the weapon once more.

"No, my brother," implored Nado. "He isn't worth it. Let the police handle everything. I need you here with me." At Nado's urging, Lil Boot relaxed his grip and let the gun slip from his hand.

"Put your hands up and place them behind your head," a policeman instructed. Lil Boot, realizing he was already in enough trouble, slowly raised his hands and placed them behind his head. He was cuffed and lifted off Kong's chest. FBI agents looked down at Kong's motionless body, amazed that he was still alive. They had called for an ambulance upon hearing gunshots. Outside, Cindy and BJ anxiously awaited news of what had transpired inside the house. When the ambulance arrived, BJ filmed the paramedics as they hurried through the front door.

"Look at this!" shouted one of the agents. Emerging from the bedroom, the agent entered the den and was astonished. Cocaine was piled high inside a massive safe, and stacks of money lined the bottom shelf. "We've just uncovered something major here," they said.

Necy's condition wasn't as bad as everyone had anticipated. The gunshot fired by Kong had merely grazed her shoulder. Paramedics treated her wound and assured her that she would be fine. Half an hour later, Nado, Lil Boot, JT, and Necy found themselves seated in separate rooms at FBI headquarters, awaiting questioning by the agents.

"My name is Agent Peterson, and this is Agent Moss. I'm sure you know why we want to talk to you," said Agent Peterson. "No, not really. Tell me why you want to talk to me," replied Nado.

"Well, first of all, we became interested in you when we heard about this free barbecue. We asked ourselves what kind of man would spend his hard-earned money to provide practically the entire city with free food and drinks. Our curiosity led us to send several agents to attend the event. We knew there must be some ulterior motive behind it. Were drugs your true objective?"

"Did you find drugs at my barbecue?" asked Nado. The agent hesitated for a moment. "No, but this could've been your unique way to recruit individuals. We know your kind knows how to outmaneuver the system," said the agent.

"Oh, you are absolutely right; I was trying to recruit people, just not for the reasons you assumed," replied Nado. "So, are you going to enlighten us on your motivations for recruiting?" asked the agent.

Nado looked at him and smiled, "Always the cunning one. You yourself admitted that you had agents planted at my barbecue, did you not? I'm sure they've reported their observations and conversations back to you. So why would you sit here questioning my integrity with such an absurd question about recruitment? Why not ask about why I left the barbecue hastily or why I went to the house where your agents found me? Why not inquire about the drugs and money discovered during their investigation? Isn't that what you really want to know?" Nado's words left the agents flustered in their seats, staring back at him in silence.

"Okay, you're right. Let's start from the beginning. We have Daniel's account of what occurred. Our goal is simply to piece everything together," said the agents. Nado sensed that the agent had finally grasped that he wasn't dealing with an uninformed man. Nado was determined to dismantle the white man's illusion of superiority over any black man, an illusion bolstered by a language inherited from his ancestors. Thoughts of 2-4 crossed Nado's mind, momentarily forgotten due to his sister's situation. He gazed intently at the agents.

"Is he alright? I didn't have time to check on him," asked Nado. "Yes, he's fine. The young lady from the stage took him to the hospital. It wasn't life-threatening – just a broken nose and some bruised ribs," the agents explained. Nado sighed with relief. "My sister, how is she?" he inquired.

"Do you mean the young lady grazed by the bullet?" asked the agent. Nado nodded. "She's physically fine in relation to the incident. Naturally, you were already aware of that. We've got agents questioning her at this moment. Hopefully, we'll have everything sorted out soon and determine our next course of action. Now, can you please walk us through today's events?" requested the agent.

Nado recounted the events that had occurred, starting with his sister's drug addiction and culminating in the invasion of Kong's residence. However, he couldn't comprehend why Kong had taken his sister. Necy filled in the missing details, and once all the information was gathered and analyzed, it led to the arrests of two individuals, Willie King (aka King Kong) and Jonathan Boothman Jr. (aka Lil Boot). Kong was charged with cocaine trafficking and kidnapping, while Lil Boot faced charges of assault and possession of an illegal firearm. After being released, Nado, JT, Necy, and 2-4 went to the county jail to post bail for Lil Boot.

Nado drove them away occasionally glancing at 2-4 through the rearview mirror, who always seemed to be watching him. Nado took everyone to his house, where each of them received a warm embrace—except for 2-4.

"Is everything alright, 2-4?" asked Nado. "You seem lost in thought. I want to thank you for your efforts today. It was very brave of you," said Nado. Mrs. Nell sat nearby, eavesdropping on their conversation. "You know," continued Nado, "I've come to appreciate your presence. Despite your past experiences, all you needed was an opportunity. You gave yourself that chance when you accepted my job offer." He glanced at his mother. "Sometimes, I think about what my dad was like or what he's like now. I'll probably never know, but I can't help but wonder. If he's anything like you 2-4, he would have been a great father," said Nado. He offered 2-4 a melancholic smile.

"Don't you go wurrin yo self-bout your daddy. You're doing well on your own, you and your sister been raised up good, dat I can see. You did wrong for a while, but you've come round. You got to help yo sista git herself back," replied 2-4, looking at Nado. "I'm sho your daddy would be proud of you." Their conversation was interrupted by the ringing of the phone. Nado got up, walked over to it, and answered the call.

"Hello, this is Na." Before he could finish, Azurie screamed into his ear, "Television! Turn on the television, quick!" Nado raced for the remote and switched on the TV. They were showing segments of his speech, edited to make him appear anti-white. Nado thought it didn't matter how white people saw him; what mattered was how his black brothers and sisters perceived him.

He heard Azurie scream and saw himself rush to the bloodied body of 2-4. The camera tried to follow him through the crowd as he, Lil Boot, and JT Dollar made their way through. "Are you still there, Nado? Are you looking at that?" asked Azurie. Nado was preoccupied with watching his car speed through the street, pursued by the FBI vehicles he had seen outside Kong's house when they were taken to the precinct. Lil Boot and JT Dollar now stood beside Nado, also watching the television.

"I'll call you back, Azurie." Before she could respond, Nado had hung up the phone and was staring again at the television. "So that's how they got to Kong's house. The television crew and the FBI had both followed us when we took off from the park," said Nado.

Lil Boot responded, "They saved his life. That's what they did. I would have beaten him so badly. I've never wanted to just annihilate anyone the way I wanted to annihilate Kong. I want to go to the hospital now and finish him off."

"You wouldn't have a chance. The feds are guarding him like Fort Knox. They found all types of fake IDs in the safe. None of them had the same name as the one in his pants pocket, but all of them had his picture," said Nado.

That aroused their curiosity. Nado continued, "The agent said that when they fingerprint him, they will get a positive identification and see just who they have. So, whether you take care of him or not, he's a dead man anyway." They watched as the medics rolled Kong out on a stretcher and put him in the ambulance. Then, they watched themselves being led to the waiting federal cars.

"I suppose Allah was watching over us today. It never fails to manifest itself in one way or another, keeping us safe. Necy was chatting with her mother in the kitchen when 2-4 entered. Mrs. Nell noticed him first and observed him closely as he approached them. Necy turned to see what had caught her mother's attention. Mrs. Nell saw Necy smile as 2-4 drew closer. "I want to thank you, Mr. Dan, for your help at the park. Your actions were truly courageous," said Necy. Before she could continue, Nado, Lil Boot, and JT joined them in the kitchen. Meanwhile, they conversed, and Nado slipped away to return Azurie's call. "I apologize for hanging up so suddenly. I wanted to watch the news on TV. Did you see how they tried to portray me as a racist?" "That's what they do, Nado when they see someone trying to make a positive change – especially a black man," said Azurie. Nado responded, "Would you like to come over? Dan is here, and we're just discussing today's events." The line went quiet. "Azurie, are you there? Did you hear my invitation?" asked Nado.

"Nado, when my father and I took your mother home today, Dan joined us. He seemed lost in his thoughts. Dan examined the pictures on the wall intently. Suddenly, your mother asked Dan if he was ready to leave. It was an odd thing for her to do. I understand Dan's background, but her rudeness made me feel embarrassed," said Azurie.

"Those are baby pictures of Necy and me in diapers. Why would he inspect them?" replied Nado.

"I don't know, but your mother's behavior made me uncomfortable," said Azurie. Nado pondered for a moment.

"Are you dressed?" asked Nado.

"Yes, why?" answered Azurie.

"I'll be there soon," Nado instructed everyone in the kitchen to wait until his return. Twenty minutes later, he and Azurie walked back through the door.

"Excuse me, everyone. Could you all please gather in the living room?" asked Nado. Everyone looked confused but obliged. "Dan, please sit in this chair here." Nado had a reason for this – the chair faced the pictures on the wall. As soon as Dan sat down, his gaze turned toward the pictures. Nado noticed his mother casting sidelong glances at him. "Mother," Nado began, "what do you think of Azurie?" The question caught Mrs. Nell off guard. She responded, "Oh, I think Azurie is a wonderful person. Why do you ask?"

"Today, when she was here, something upset her. She feels that you come across as rude. Were you rude, Mother? Why would she think that?" asked Nado.

Mrs. Nell looked at Azurie, who met her gaze directly. "I don't understand, Azurie. I didn't think I did anything rude to you today. There was so much going on that I could have done something unintentionally, but I would never purposely hurt anyone's feelings. I apologize if I did," said Mrs. Nell.

"No, I never said you were rude to me. It was Dan that you were rude to. After he got beaten up trying to help Necy today, you treated him like he wasn't welcome in your home – as if you were afraid, he might steal something. It just made me wonder if you'd treat me the same way," said Azurie. Mrs. Nell wanted to clear Azurie's mind quickly, but her words only reinforced Azurie's assumptions.

"This house has a man in it. I..." Mrs. Nell stopped mid-sentence, realizing she had misspoken. As Nado turned away from Dan, who was intently studying the pictures, he looked at her with a puzzled expression. Mrs. Nell lowered her head. "I'm sorry," she said, tears welling up in her eyes. Nado approached and held her at arm's length.

"What's wrong, Mother? Why did you say this house has a man in it? What does that have to do with you being rude to Dan?" Nado inquired. Mrs. Nell shook her head and fled the room. Dan sat back, reflecting on the situation. Had he not come to this house, everything would be fine now. The name he had overheard at the barbecue piqued his curiosity, prompting him to investigate and satisfy the strange feeling gnawing at him. But his curiosity had transformed what should have been a simple seek-and-find mission into a disastrous situation.

"I don't feel good," Dan said, "I'd like to go back to my room." Without saying another word, he lowered his head and walked towards the front door.

"Do you understand why I said what I said now?" asked Azurie. "I have a strange feeling that something isn't right," Nado replied, standing next to Azurie while gazing at the pictures on the wall.

"I'll take Dan to his room, but in the meantime, I need you to stay here with Mom and make sure she's okay. I don't know what it is, but something is definitely off here," Nado said. He bent down and gently placed his first kiss on Azurie's cheek, then stepped back to observe her reaction. The beautiful smile that had captured him when they first met greeted him once more. She reached out and touched Nado's hand.

"Hurry back," said Azurie. Azurie turned and followed the path Mrs. Nell had taken. Nado went outside to where Lil Boot and JT had gone. "I'll be back shortly. If you have anything to do, go ahead and handle it." Nado started to walk away but stopped. He began to speak but was interrupted by Lil Boot. "No need to say it, Nado. What's understood doesn't need explaining," said Lil Boot. Nado nodded and walked to his car, where 2-4 was waiting. They began their ride in silence, with 2-4 gazing out the window, observing the neighborhood. Nado wanted 2-4 to share what was bothering him but didn't want to push. The silence persisted until Nado couldn't stand it anymore.

"Hey 2-4, is there anything you want to talk about?" 2-4 slowly turned to face Nado. "Ever done something that you ever regret?" I mean, really regret?" Nado replied, "Who hasn't? We've all done things we regret."

"Sometimes people do stuff without thinking about who dey is gonna hurt. It brings a lot of pain in other folks' lives. I heard you up there on dat stage talking bout being strong and having second chances. Do you really believe dat everyone deserves another chance no matter what dey done?" asked 2-4. Nado thought for a moment. "Yes, everyone deserves a chance if they can change their ways," replied Nado. "Naw, that ain't what I mean. If-in you did something one-time dat was really bad, and you hurt some peoples on the way, do you think that dey could forgive you?" asked 2-4. Nado knew that 2-4 was referring to something from his own life, so he needed to be cautious in his response.

"Well, it really depends on what I did. Do you have a family, 2-4?" Nado noticed that his question took 2-4 by surprise. Instead of answering, 2-4 just stared out the window until they arrived at his room. As 2-4 got out of the car, Nado watched him walk towards the room. When 2-4 reached for the door, he turned back to face Nado. Nado rolled down his window to hear what 2-4 had to say. "A long time ago," was all 2-4 said before he turned and entered his room.

Azurie stood near the foot of the bed, observing Necy comforting Mrs. Nell. She had regained composure after their abrupt exit from the living room.

"Could you fetch me a glass of water, dear?" asked Mrs. Nell. Necy obliged and left the room. Mrs. Nell turned to Azurie and locked eyes with her. Azurie thought to herself, "Here it comes; I knew she wouldn't let me off the hook for telling Nado about her behavior today. Let her say her piece, and from then on, I'll just keep my distance."

"Are you alright, Mrs. Nell?" inquired Azurie. To her surprise, a melancholic smile formed on Mrs. Nell's face. "I apologize if I came across as rude today," said Mrs. Nell. Azurie sensed that something was troubling her; perhaps if she could encourage Mrs. Nell to open up, they could resolve the issue. Azurie walked around the bed to sit beside her, taking her hands gently. As she looked at Mrs. Nell, she noticed a tear lingering on her chin from its descent down her cheek.

"I am an excellent listener, Mrs. Nell," Azurie said, sensing that she needed someone to talk to. Perhaps she had been mistaken about Mrs. Nell, but either way, Azurie wanted to give her the opportunity to speak her mind.

"Do you know how difficult it is to raise two children on your own?" Mrs. Nell asked, her gaze fixed on Azurie. "I've done everything in my power to ensure they have everything they need. I've always been honest with them." She paused before continuing, "Have you ever had a secret? Not a trivial one – I mean a secret that could expose things best left hidden. I would give my life to protect my children."

CHAPTER TWELVE

Echoes of Redemption: The Dexter's Final Reckoning

While Mrs. Nell and Azurie were talking, they failed to notice Necy's return as she stood silently near the half-opened door, eavesdropping on their conversation.

"I don't know how much Nado has told you about our family, but I need to talk to someone. Long ago, when Nado and Necy were just kids, their father got involved in drugs. At first, I didn't know what was going on until he confessed his problem to me. We tried to overcome his addiction together, but it overwhelmed him. He began wasting our bill money, which left me with less time to spend at home with our kids. Instead of both of us caring for them, it became only me supporting our three children – their father seemed like another child. One day, while I was at work, he left a note saying he was doing more harm than good and wouldn't return until he conquered his addiction. He never came back. As days turned into months and months into years, I had to accept the fact that the man I loved had turned his back on us. I often wondered if he was alright or had gotten himself killed.

Despite being exhausted from long hours of work, I played with the kids every night until we all passed out from tiredness. Without my neighbor, Mrs. Lee, I don't think I could have handled everything – she took pictures of us playing together, and I hung them on the wall for motivation. Eventually, I hoped he'd stay gone, but he didn't. It's a secret I've kept for thirteen years.

I remember the day he returned as if it were yesterday. He appeared before me, unrecognizable except for his eyes. That day, I cried a river in the kitchen, thinking of all the years he'd been absent, even on birthdays. When Nado saw me crying and asked what was wrong, all I could say was that I was tired from working – this lie changed his life instantly as he decided it was time to care for me as I had cared for him and Necy," said Mrs. Nell.

Mrs. Nell paused, giving Azurie a moment to ask the question that was on her mind. "You mentioned that no one recognized your husband. How could that be? Didn't people know him around town?" asked Azurie.

"Oh sure, practically everyone knew him. He was very handsome and well-groomed. All the ladies had their eyes on him, but I was the lucky one. I walked proudly while others whispered and scoffed. I thought all I needed was his and our children's love. But when I saw him again, he had changed. He dressed poorly; his hair was long, and he wore torn and dirty clothes. You've seen him many times yourself, Azurie, and I'm sure you know his name," said Mrs. Nell.

Azurie responded, "Did you ever tell your children their father's name?"

"You have to remember, Azurie; they were just kids when he left us — innocent children depending on their parents to guide them into adulthood. By the time they were old enough to understand the situation, his name became a distant memory. No, I didn't tell them their father's name, and I wish I never had to reveal it. However, I'm not sure if I can keep this secret any longer. If things had been different when I saw him three years ago, maybe I could have told them," Mrs. Nell said.

Azurie seemed to lose hope. "I guess the drugs must have turned him into the person who approached me."

"I don't know who or what he is now, and all I could think about was his children being ashamed of their father's transformation. As Mrs. Nell continued to talk, Necy quietly stood outside the bedroom door, listening. She was no longer alone. Necy had initially returned with her mother's water and began eavesdropping upon hearing the conversation between her mother and Azurie. Just as she heard the front door close, she knew it had to be Nado. She intercepted him in the hallway before he reached their mother's room and explained the situation. Together, they silently returned to their mother's door and listened."

"Mrs. Nell, do you think they have the right to know who their father is? They've suffered without him for years, but they had a strong woman to minimize that suffering. They're adults now, capable of love, understanding, and accepting whatever they choose. Just because they don't talk about their father doesn't mean they don't wonder who he is, where he is, or what he's like. They deserve the right to know and share your anger if they choose," said Azurie.

Mrs. Nell responded, "I know what you're saying is true, but it's hard. Do you think they'll be upset with me for not telling them when I first saw him? I only wanted to protect them; that's all I ever wanted." Mrs. Nell looked at Azurie. "Why haven't you asked me his name?" Azurie smiled at Mrs. Nell and squeezed her hand. "You've kept this inside for so long. You'll reveal his name when you're ready." Mrs. Nell smiled back at Azurie.

"I guess I'm as ready as I'll ever be, but I may need a little help. I just prayed that my children understand why I didn't tell them when I first saw him again. They sat in silence for a moment until it was broken by three words: 'Daniel Dexter,' their father's name," said Mrs. Nell.

Azurie's surprised look turned into a startled expression as she and Mrs. Nell faced the sound of breaking glass. Outside the bedroom door, Necy stood with her hand over her mouth, stunned in disbelief at the words she had just heard from her mother. Meanwhile, Nado remained motionless, staring down at the shattered glass that had slipped from his sister's hand.

"Well, if I ever had a second thought about leaving all this behind, today wiped them clean," Lil Boot declared a glint of determination in his eyes. JT nodded, his expression mirroring Lil Boot's sentiment. "You know, Lil Boot, I can't help but feel the same way. After all the chaos that went down at Kong's place, I'd bet my last dollar they're gonna start asking questions, poking around in the snitches' business. And you know where that leads, right?"

"Look at it like this, man," JT continued, his tone contemplative. "We've come a long way from when we started this gig. We set goals and deadlines for ourselves, and by far, we met them all. We've seen it all, nearly done it all. We've got a stash of cash saved up, and once we offload the rest of our goods, we'll be set for life."

Lil Boot leaned with a spark of excitement in his eyes. "I've got an idea, JT. This new path we're on goes against everything Nado's trying to do if we let this stuff hit the streets."

JT raised an eyebrow in skepticism. "Hell no, Lil Boot. I'm not going back on this. But go on, lay it out."

Lil Boot leaned back, considering his words carefully. "Remember that dude Necy mentioned? The one who got her hooked-on smoking? Boss Player, right?"

JT nodded slowly, still unsure where this was going. "Yeah, but what's he got to do with all of this?"

Lil Boot grinned slyly. "Doesn't he have a little cash saved up? Doesn't he have friends who've got some too? What if we give him a call, set up a meeting, and tell him we're bowing out of the game? We'll sweeten the deal for him, lay all our cards on the table."

JT scratched his chin, mulling over the idea. "Man, Lil Boot, do you even realize how much we've got left? That guy might have some cheddar, but he ain't even close to moving the kind of product we've got."

Lil Boot leaned in; his eyes gleaming with confidence. "I know, JT, but sometimes it's not about the quantity; it's about the connections. And Boss Player might just have the right ones to help us make a smooth exit from this game."

"Exactly, that's my point. He has joined forces with some more ballers, and that will take time. That will also give me time to inform Nado about a large stash of drugs," said JT.

Lil Boot responded, "Okay, now I understand. We take our cut and then turn Nado loose on them. Hurt him financially for what he did to Necy." "Not bad, not bad at all." They sat in silence for a moment.

JT Dollar changed the subject, "Hey partner, do you regret what happened today? I mean, what happened with Kong?"

Lil Boot replied, "I should have killed his weak ass twice. Is it visiting hours at the hospital?" "I didn't think so," said JT while pausing briefly before continuing, "Well, what are you waiting for? Are you going to make that call or what?"

Lil Boot took out his address book, got Boss Player's number, and dialed it into his phone.

"Yeah, this is Boss. What's up?"

"What's up, Boss; this is Lil Boot. I need to talk to you." The phone went silent. Boss Player had seen on the television what had happened to Kong and knew that he was talking to the man responsible for it.

"Hey, I had nothing to do with that shit," said Boss Player. "Wait a minute. What are you talking about?" Lil Boot smiled and winked at JT Dollar, knowing exactly what Boss was referring to.

"I saw it on TV, man. I had nothing to do with Kong taking Necy," Boss Player continued. Lil Boot replied, "That's not why I need to see you. You already said you didn't know Necy. Why would you think you were involved? That's been handled. If I thought for even a second that you were part of today's events, we wouldn't be talking over the phone."

"Alright, as long as you know, I wasn't involved. So, what do you want to discuss with Boss?" Lil Boot responded, "Coffee shop in fifteen minutes." He then ended the call. The boss sat still, staring at his silent phone. At least they didn't want to kill him. Maybe Necy hadn't mentioned anything about him. He got up, put on his shoes, and left.

Azurie went outside to find Nado after hearing the news. There was nothing she could say at that moment; she could only offer her comfort. Nado looked up at Azurie's sad smile.

"Hell of a bomb, wasn't it, huh? I never would have thought Dan could be our father in a million years," Nado said. "You know, I understand why mom did what she did, but it doesn't make it any easier. That's why he kept looking at those pictures on the wall – that's when he left." Nado stood up and continued talking to Azurie: "I need to hear it from him – how a man can just abandon his wife and little kids. I'd like for you to come too. This family will finally sit down together, and Dan will have to explain himself." Nado went inside and approached his mother. Mrs. Nell embraced her son, burying her head in his chest.

"I'm so sorry, Nado. I just didn't know what to do," Azurie apologized. Mrs. Nell began to cry once more. "Don't cry, Mother. It's time for you to find closure, and it's time for Necy and me to get some long-awaited answers," Nado asserted. He told Necy to get dressed, and moments later, they were in Nado's sleek black BMW, driving towards Dan's motel room.

2-4 spotted the car as it pulled up in front of his room. The million-dollar question was about to be answered. Before Nado could knock, 2-4 opened the door and welcomed them inside.

Once inside, Nado stared at Dan, bewildered. The disheveled man he had grown fond of was none other than his long-lost father – Daniel Dexter.

"Where should I begin?" asked Mrs. Nell. The question stirred the suppressed anger that had settled deep within her, momentarily making her forget the recent scene in her home. She could still recognize remnants of the man she once loved in Dan's face, but time had taken its toll on his appearance. Swallowing hard, she stood directly in front of Dan.

"I waited countless nights for you to come home, Dan. Those nights turned into years, and eventually, I realized you weren't coming back. I often held our children as they slept, wishing their father would walk through the door, but you never did. Did you ever wonder how we were doing? Did you ever consider how difficult it was for me to raise two children alone? Why didn't you ever come home? I can accept that you never returned; I just think after all these years, I deserve to know why. Can you tell me that?" Mrs. Nell asked earnestly.

Feeling a weight of eyes upon him, 2-4 scanned the room before meeting Mrs. Nell's gaze.

"I know that nothing I say here can make up for what I've done. Nado and Necy, I want you to know I've loved you since the moment you were born. My addiction to drugs consumed me, and no matter how hard I tried, they always overpowered me. As my addiction worsened, I became increasingly useless, neglecting work and wasting money. Your mother tried to help, but she couldn't save me from my downward spiral.

My friends criticized both me and your mother, making things unbearable until, inevitably, I felt that leaving you all behind was the best way to help. Once gone, I wandered aimlessly from place to place, too intoxicated to remember anything. To avoid recognition, I grew long hair and changed my appearance.

I gradually adapted to life on the streets, facing overwhelming loneliness as the years passed by. Eventually, surviving an overdose led me to kick my drug habit, clearing my mind and sparking thoughts of reconnecting with you all. Uncertain of whether your appearance had changed since our last encounter and with no way of knowing how you and Necy looked now, I retained images of you in my mind similar to photos from your house.

Finally driven by homesickness, I returned, unrecognizable in my old clothes and long hair. Nell's face captivated me upon our first encounter after so long; however, accidentally confronting her only sent her running away in fear like she had seen a ghost. Though we crossed paths a few times afterward, I never dared approach her again.

Fate allowed me to meet you that night at the dumpster without recognizing each other as father and son. When we went to the barbecue and heard your name – Alvernado

Dexter – everything clicked into place for me. Reflecting upon Necy's chin scar sustained under my care served as further confirmation.

Unexpectedly welcomed into your home one day, fate unveiled the truth. Azurie didn't understand my connection to your family and assumed I was simply a homeless man in need, which was accurate." Dan paused before proceeding while Azurie offered him a sympathetic smile. "It was merely my destiny to become entwined with you all."

Dan turned to Necy. "It takes a desperate man to leave his wife and children, and seeing you today, I can't help but feel the pain you're going through. You haven't reached the point of no return like I did, but out of everyone here, I know you're the one who might understand why I chose to leave. Should I have stayed? It's easy for me to say yes now because my mind is no longer clouded by drugs."

He faced the others. "If you've never experienced it, you can't comprehend the struggle. I didn't return to interfere in anyone's life; I relinquished that right when I left you all to fend for yourselves. It was only by the grace of God that your mother was strong enough to raise you well without me. I'll be leaving town again soon, as I have no intention of disrupting your lives any further."

"You're what?" Nado asked in an authoritative voice. "Is this how you adapt to life when facing adversity? Just run and hope everything eventually disappears? Well, I guess you're not the person I thought I knew after all. Let's go." Without another word, Nado, Azurie, and the rest of the Dexter family turned and walked out of the room. This time, the tables were turned as Dan watched his family walk away. On the drive back to the Dexter's house, not a single word was spoken; each member was lost in their own thoughts.

Several days later, no one had seen or heard from Dan. He stopped making his usual morning visits to McDonald's, and Azurie genuinely began to miss him. Nado launched his "reclaim our community" initiative, and within a few days, he and his team of recruits, led by his top men, Lil Boot and JT Dollar, convinced several local drug dealers that changing their profession would be in their best interest. Occasionally, the community's friends had to make a late-night visit to remind dealers who continued their old ways that they held a special place in the community and deserved extra attention. Usually, it only took a bit of persuasive conversation from JT and Lil Boot to change their minds.

Many members of the community's friends were young black men whose lives had been impacted by drugs. Their parents or someone close to them had been affected by addiction. They all looked up to Nado and respected his efforts. They patrolled the neighborhoods in shifts, wearing shirts provided by Nado to signal their presence and unity.

Whenever someone encountered a problem that couldn't be resolved, they simply paged Nado and his team for help. As the community observed the progress of the "friends of our community," more people began to join their ranks.

Parents became more attentive to their children's activities, and children paid closer attention to their parents' actions as they now had someone who cared about their lives. Nado emerged as a force to be reckoned with.

"You have the right to remain silent. Anything you say can be used against you." Kong listened as the FBI agent read him his rights. Awakening from a week-long semi-coma, he lay in bed, trying to recall how he ended up there. Suddenly, the entire incident replayed in his mind. He could see himself falling as Necy crashed into him, and Lil Boot's pistol struck his head.

Upon his release from the hospital, federal agents immediately arrested him for kidnapping and cocaine trafficking. Three days later, while aimlessly wandering the infirmary ward, he heard his name on the intercom: "Willie King, report to the cubicle." He hadn't been called Willie King since leaving Queens, New York, three years prior. Was an old partner here to post his bond? With all his money confiscated from his safe by the feds, he would have to rely on old associates.

He wanted to use the telephone to contact someone and explain his situation. Smiling, he approached the cubicle. When he arrived, he couldn't believe who was waiting for him – a couple of old friends from Queens. However, they weren't there with good news; instead, they handed him a piece of paper and grinned. These friends were federal agents, the very reason he had left his home base in the first place.

"We've been looking for you, Willie. Look, we brought you a little gift." They informed him of his rights, presented the warrant and indictment for conspiring to distribute cocaine, and charged him under the RICO Act. All hope that Kong had vanished instantly as he realized this would be his new home for the foreseeable future.

Nado had become a highly sought-after figure. News stations from across the United States sent out their top reporters to interview him. His biggest draw was an all-expenses-paid trip to appear on various news outlets. High-ranking media members would personally conduct these interviews. In anticipation of each appearance, the news channel announced the identities and schedules of their special guests daily. They frequently aired footage of Nado's barbecue speech, focusing primarily on what seemed to be racially charged segments. This sparked mixed emotions among the public, ensuring that everyone would tune in to learn more about this enigmatic young man.

"I want you to travel with me and sit on the set with me," Nado said. Minister Malik Shakur nodded his head in understanding. Nado had been attending the mosque and learning the teachings of the Honorable Elijah Muhammad from Minister Malik Shakur. He was very impressed by Nado's desire to learn more. Initially, he had doubted Nado's sincerity but was convinced after hearing him speak at a barbecue and seeing his work for the black community. With Nado's help, he could experience places he would have never considered visiting. It would be an honor to accompany this young man.

"Nado paused, his gaze resting on Minister Malik Shakur. "I presume you would like my daughter to join us as well?" he asked. His thoughts then drifted to his daughter and the profound influence she had on his life. "It was during our first date when I realized her strength," he began, his tone filled with respect. "She told me she couldn't see me again. It wasn't because of anything I had done or said. Instead, it was due to her principles, instilled in her through her upbringing."

Nado had grown to respect her stance, particularly as he was willing to offer her the world at the time. He admired her refusal to base her life on material wealth, instead opting for a life guided by ethics. The sight of her paying for her own meal, Nado realized, should have been his first clue to her independent spirit.

He halted his reminiscence abruptly, the memories of his father, Dan, becoming too overwhelming. Dealing with Dan's absence was challenging for Nado. He had grown accustomed to his presence, and discovering his true nature had left him disoriented. Dan had been gone for some time now, but Nado often found himself wondering about his whereabouts and well-being.

To distract himself from these thoughts, Nado immersed himself in various neighborhood activities. Occasionally, during his neighborhood patrols, he would unconsciously gravitate towards the dumpster - the place where he had first encountered his father. He secretly hoped to catch a glimpse of him there, just like old times. But he had to accept the harsh reality - his father had once again done what he'd done years ago. He had left him.

"I'm aware. Azurie told me everything," Minister Shakur replied. His gaze turned serious as he asked, "Have you seen him lately?" Nado shook his head in response. "Would you like to see him again?"

Nado hesitated, contemplating the question. "To see him again?" he echoed, his voice indicating uncertainty. He paused again before elaborating, "When I first met him, he was just a homeless man to me, albeit an exceptionally intelligent one. As I spent more time with him, I grew fond of him. Then, to discover that he was my father... it stirred a whirlwind of emotions within me. But because I got to know him on my own terms, it made the revelation somewhat easier to accept."

"Do I want to see him again? I'm conflicted. Part of me yearns for it, while the other part feels you can't miss what you never had," Nado confessed. He looked at Minister Shakur, adding, "In a way, I do miss him. But it doesn't matter now. He's gone, once again."

Sensing Nado's emotional unrest, Minister Shakur gently steered the conversation toward a lighter topic. He spoke about the growing congregation at his mosque, attributing the increase to Nado's inspiring message.

"Son, I want you to know that I had my doubts about you, but I stand corrected," Minister Shakur admitted. "Please feel free to reach out to me if you ever need to talk," Nado responded with a smile and a salute.

"Regarding Azurie," Nado began, "you never confirmed if she could accompany us." Minister Shakur grinned at Nado's inquiry. "And you, my son, never asked!" Their shared laughter echoed in the room. "Yes, she's welcome to join us," Minister Shakur confirmed. Nado noticed the emphasis he placed on 'us.' "I'll inform her of the decision tonight," he added.

Nado expressed his gratitude, "Thank you, Minister. As-Salaam Alaikum." Minister Shakur responded warmly, "Wa-Alaikum-Salaam."

As Nado was about to leave, his phone rang. "Hello, this is Nado. How may I assist you?" he answered.

"We've got a big one," Lil Boot's voice crackled through the phone. "I mean, as big as it gets. We're at the park."

"I'm on my way," Nado replied promptly.

Lil Boot shared a triumphant smile with JT over stacks of money. Boss Player, having collaborated with several contacts, managed to gather enough money to buy out the remainder of Lil Boot and JT's supply.

The shipment was scheduled to be delivered to Boss Player's house at exactly 7 pm. Then, at 7:15 pm, the community friends would pay them a visit. But Lil Boot had a more elaborate plan. He had promised Cindy, an ambitious reporter, an exclusive story on the community friends' action against drug activity. In return, he wanted positive press, emphasizing their determination to eradicate drug problems in the community.

Lil Boot suggested that if Cindy had any contacts in the department who could ensure non-interference with their operations, they could stake out the location. After the community friends had completed their mission, they could take over the scene.

After a considerable discussion, Cindy's contact agreed to the proposal. She immediately relayed the approval to Lil Boot.

Cindy then called her top-notch cameraman, BJ who

promptly left his ongoing assignment to meet her at the station. With only ten minutes left, they prepared to leave.

At exactly 7 pm, the bell at Boss Player's house rang. The drop was made in just two minutes. The occupants of the house instantly began unwrapping the package.

"Is everything accounted for?" Boss Player inquired; his attention focused on the neatly stacked blocks of cocaine. Suddenly, the front and back doors of the house burst open. Caught off guard, the occupants of the house had no time to react as the friends of the community swiftly moved in, blocking all potential escape routes and securing the hands of everyone present.

Trailing behind them was BJ with his camera sweeping the scene. Cindy had instructed him to capture the decisive actions of the friends of the community and the stunned expressions of the men they apprehended. Naturally, BJ also captured footage of the cocaine stash, which would be handed over to the task force.

Once the situation was under control, Lil Boot signaled Cindy, who stepped outside to alert her friend in the task force. BJ kept his camera rolling as the task force stormed into the house, guns at the ready. However, they found there was little for them to do. The friends of the community had already neutralized the situation effectively.

The commander of the force approached Nado, who met his gaze unflinchingly. The camera zoomed in as they stood face to face. Nado nodded at the commander before turning to his team, "Let's go." He stepped aside, allowing each member of his team to exit the premises.

Before leaving, Nado walked over to Boss Player. He stood before him, his expression stern. "You contributed to the corruption that harmed my sister, Necy. Know that Allah always protects His children. Now, it's Allah's turn to deal with you." With that, Nado turned and walked away, leaving Boss Player to his fate.

By 10 pm, every household in the community had tuned in to the local news. If there had been any doubts before about the community friends and their ability to enact change, tonight's broadcast was sure to put those doubts to rest.

As the town was engrossed in the news, Nado and Azurie were taking a leisurely drive through the countryside. Nado had filled Azurie in on the evening's events and mentioned that it would be featured on the 10 pm news. But Azurie, being the kind of person she was, didn't need to see the television broadcast to believe in Nado's commitment to truth and justice.

"What do you think of me, Azurie?" Nado asked, his question catching her by surprise. She had anticipated it, knowing it was inevitable. Throughout their time together, Nado had been nothing less than a gentleman. He had shown affection towards her sparingly, with the exception of a single kiss on the cheek. Nevertheless, it was undeniable that they had grown quite fond of each other.

Azurie turned to look at Nado. "Nado, you already know the answer to that. You've known it since the moment I accepted your dinner invitation." She smiled at him gently, adding, "You know you hurt me that day, don't you?"

Nado pulled the car over to the side of the road. "I'll never hurt you again," he promised. Leaning towards Azurie, they met halfway, sharing their first kiss under the moonlit sky.

After the kiss, Nado straightened up in his seat, a contented smile on his face. "I should get you home," he said. The drive home was serene, their hands entwined, both lost in thoughts of the memorable kiss they had just shared.

On the following day, they prepared to embark on their mission. "We eagerly anticipate your return," voiced Mrs. Nell. Except for Necy, the whole community assembled at the airport to bid their farewell. Prior to this, Nado had discussed his concerns about Necy's need for professional help. They had mutually decided that she would check into a rehabilitation center a day before his departure.

Since her rescue from Kong's house, Necy had been stable. Not once had she attempted to escape from her home. Nado's only wish was for her to come to terms with the events that had transpired in her life.

2-4, on the other hand, had used the money Nado gave him to travel to South Carolina. He found himself in a modest motel room where he now sat, engrossed in the national news. The image on the screen left him stunned. The young man he had come to consider his son was being interviewed by Connie Chung in a television studio. Overcome with excitement, 2-4 nearly tripped in his haste to increase the television volume, managing just in time to catch the beginning of the interview.

"Good evening, I'm Connie Chung, and tonight we have a special guest, Mr. Alvernado Dexter," she began. The camera panned to Nado, who greeted the audience with a warm smile. "Mr. Dexter has rapidly emerged into the public eye, and you're about to witness his first, and certainly not his last, exclusive interview here on Dateline. Mr. Dexter, would you mind sharing with our viewers what you aim to achieve?"

"Peace be upon you, in the name of Allah, the Beneficent, the Merciful. I testify that there is no one worthy of worship except Allah, and I confirm that Muhammad is His messenger. To respond to your question, it's important to clarify that I, as an individual, am not aiming to achieve anything. This mission is far greater than a single person. I am merely a voice for the people.

What we, in the Nation of Islam, are striving for is the resurrection, redemption, and restoration of the Black man, woman, and child. We are attempting to awaken our people from a 400-year-old slumber during which our identity, language, and religion were stripped away. We seek the fulfillment of the Bible, which speaks of the Day of Resurrection - the awakening of the mentally dead. And, unfortunately, this description of being 'mentally dead' fits none better than the Black man and woman in America."

"Mr. Dexter, your words may lead some viewers to believe that you are attempting to stir up racial tensions between the Black and White communities. Is this your intention?"

"The Nation of Islam cannot be accused of inciting racial tensions between the Black and White communities. You must understand that the Nation only came into being in the 1930s, while America has existed for a much longer period. America is a country whose foundation is deeply rooted in racism. Even some of the founding fathers of this great nation owned Black slaves.

From its inception, America has operated under a belief system based on white supremacy. This belief system permeates every institution in America, including the church, politics, the judiciary, education, and the economy. Blacks were legally emancipated from slavery in 1865, yet the lynching of Black individuals continues to this day. The Black community had to fight for the passage of civil rights bills just to secure the right to vote. Time and time again, they had to rely on these civil rights bills to gain basic rights.

You see, racial tension has always been here. What kind of bills did the White community have to pass to secure their right to vote? As long as there exists a relationship akin to that of a slave and a slave master, peace between the two communities is impossible, as it contradicts human nature.

Let me illustrate this with a simple example from nature. Have you ever observed ducks or geese flying south for the winter? You would never see a buzzard or an eagle flying alongside them. Humans are supposed to be superior to all other creatures on Earth, yet birds have the sense to stick with their own kind.

The principles of who the original man was have been replaced by the white slave master's inferiority complex. This leads people to believe that they don't deserve better.

Now, allow me to pose a question to you, Mrs. Chung. Which is better: a slave master who drives his slaves to the field on a wagon, allows them to start work at 7:30, provides them with water breaks, and lets them stop working at 3:30, transporting them back to the plantation by wagon? Or a slave master who demands his slaves rise before sunrise, walk to the field, begin work as soon as the sun peaks the hill, offers no water, and makes them work until dark, then berates them on their walk home for not doing enough? Which slave master, in your opinion, is better?"

"Mr. Dexter, I believe most people would opt for the slave master who allows for specific work hours and provides water," Mrs. Chung responded. Nado countered, "That's where you're mistaken, Mrs. Chung. A slave master is a slave master; none are better than the other. One merely employs psychological manipulation to create the illusion of better treatment. The slaves who work certain hours and receive water become complacent and comfortable, fearing being sold to a harsher master, while those who are treated poorly will eventually tire of the abuse and escape. This is just another form of the white man's trickery. We are here to dispel such ignorance."

"We'll be back after the commercial," announced Mrs. Chung. During the break, Nado exchanged reassuring smiles with Minister Shakur, Azurie, and his two best friends as the countdown resumed: 3-2-1.

"For those of you tuning in, we are joined by a special guest, Mr. Alvernado Dexter. Mr. Dexter, what are your thoughts on interracial relationships or marriages?" Mrs. Chung asked.

Nado replied, "We do not support interracial relationships or marriages. We believe that the original people, or the Black man, should be of his own kind. While we are all part of the human race, we are clearly not the same people. You don't see a lion mating with a tiger, even though they belong to the cat family. Nature informs them that they are of different breeds. So why should humans act any differently?"

Mrs. Chung posed a question, "You're always surrounded by people, particularly the two young men accompanying you today, Jonathan Boothman and Jerry Tyrome Dollar, captured by our cameras. Are they your bodyguards? Have you received threats that necessitate such protection?"

The statement was deeply impactful, "We are united in a genuine brotherhood, as instructed by the Quran, which emphasizes the importance of believers safeguarding each other. Voicing the truth, particularly as a black man, is often misconstrued as a challenge to a system that thrives on deceptions. This nation's past is marred by not just scare tactics, but also by the elimination of influential black men who aimed to free their people. Eminent figures like The Most Honorable Elijah Muhammad and Minister Louis Farrakhan were not just subjected to threats but were also on the hit list for assassination. However, their adversaries were unsuccessful. Any individual who follows these esteemed men and subscribes to their teachings can be seen as their personal protectors. Picture the sheer count of such 'protectors.' Our teachings instill in us the fear of only Allah. Much like a prudent man guards his treasures, teachers of Islam, who are indeed treasures themselves, are bound to be, and indeed will be, shielded."

Mrs. Chung pressed on, "Mr. Dexter, you've pledged to gather a robust group of black men and women to reclaim your communities from drug dealers. Will you employ force to achieve this?"

Nado replied, "The only force we need is the divine backing we receive when standing for truth. We understand why our people have adopted the mindset that propels them into drug peddling. It's this mindset we aim to rectify with love, understanding, and strength. Drug dealing only breeds destruction and imprisonment, weakening our black community. We mustn't be likened to the devil's army that destroys for the sake of wealth. Our mission is to save lives and heal our people."

Mrs. Chung asked, "Do you believe the black communities will respond to your call?" Nado, smiling at the camera, answered, "They have. They already have."

Wrapping up the interview, Mrs. Chung said, "Thank you for joining us tonight. We wish you success in achieving your goal. This has been an exclusive from Dateline."

Nado interjected, "May I have one more moment?" Not waiting for Mrs. Chung's response, knowing they were still live on the air, he added, "I want to speak to all the black men watching tonight. Family is important. Regardless of past mistakes, today is a new day. If there's one thing Allah blessed the original people with, it's humility. Thank you for having me. As-salamu alaykum. Peace be unto you."

Following the broadcast, the station was inundated with calls from viewers of all races and genders, all eager to contact Alvernado Dexter. The influx of calls continued into the early morning, prompting the station to provide Nado's contact details during an extra segment the following evening.

Back in his hometown, residents watched the show with pride. Their local hero was on national television, and the town was buzzing. Neighbors and friends had called each other, reminding them to tune in to watch Nado.

Meanwhile, 2-4 sat in a small hotel room, reflecting on his life. He regretted his past involvement with drugs and wished he had been stronger. He pondered how his children could possibly want a father who had abandoned them as infants. As he was about to fall asleep, he glanced at the muted television. To his astonishment, he saw his son, Nado, looking directly at him. He quickly turned up the volume just in time to hear the host introduce Nado.

As he listened to his son speak, 2-4 laid back, daydreaming about the people he had come to know as his son and daughter. His reverie was broken by his son's voice from the television. Nado's words carried a message that cut deep into 2-4's heart, making him do something he hadn't done in a long time - he wept. Stirred by his emotions, 2-4 got up, put on his shoes, and prepared to take action. There was no time to waste.

On the journey home, Nado was lost in thought. Azurie noticed his preoccupation, aware that it was likely about his father, who had once again departed. Nado rarely spoke about his father, but when he did, Azurie could sense his growing affection for the man he'd only recently discovered was his parent. She understood that Nado had evolved from the man she first met into someone with a clear purpose and ambition.

Gently touching Nado, she brought him back to the present. They exchanged tender smiles. "Are you okay?" Azurie asked. After a brief pause, Nado admitted, "Just thinking about 2-4. I can understand why he left. After discovering his true identity, we probably made him feel unwelcome. I suppose it hurts because I got to know him as a man before knowing he was my father." Azurie optimistically added, "Maybe he'll come back and visit us one day."

Minister Shakur later discussed with Nado, Lil Boot, and JT the surprising turnout of young black males and females at mass. Most attendees stated their belief in Nado's cause as their reason for attending.

Once home, Nado was greeted warmly by everyone. Whether they knew him personally or had seen him on television, his goal had been achieved, and he was pleased with the progress made in such a short time. His days were filled with tasks, and thanks to Azurie and his family, his evenings were equally busy, reinforcing the impact he had made on his community.

"Necy was just a few weeks away from completing her drug rehabilitation program, and she maintained high spirits. She and Nado occasionally discussed their father, but it was a sensitive topic. However, one thing was certain - they both missed him in their unique ways.

"Who is it?" Mrs. Nell inquired, squinting through the peephole. Her heart seemed to pause as she peered into the face of the man who had once been a ghost in her life. "What do you want?" she demanded more than asked, her voice echoing through the closed door. Yet, she found herself unlocking the door almost involuntarily. Now, she and the man who had deserted her years ago stood alone, their gazes locked. Dan was no longer the ragged figure they had once labeled him as. He now resembled his younger, more vibrant self."

Dan remained silent; his gaze locked onto Mrs. Nell. "Speak up," she urged, "You've resurfaced for a reason. Out with it." Dan swallowed, then began, "Nellie, I've apologized for the pain I caused you and the kids, but I know it's not enough. I can't undo my past mistakes, and I don't expect your forgiveness. I need nothing from you. You've raised two admirable children alone.

I understand you want no part of me, and I don't blame you. But I need to speak to the children to see if they might give me another chance. If they refuse, it'll hurt, but I would deserve it. I can't disappear again without knowing where I stand. I hope you can understand that."

Dan fell silent, anxious under Mrs. Nell's steady, unblinking stare. "You hurt me, Dan," she admitted. "I once loved you deeply, but that love evaporated with your actions. I transferred all my love for you to our children. Now, I feel nothing for you. The kids are fine, and they can handle themselves now."

Mrs. Nell's face softened into a small smile as she invited Dan in. "Just to be clear," she said, reaching for the phone, "Your presence here is solely for the children. There's no 'us.' You ensured that when you left. Are we clear before I call Nado?"

Dan gave a nod and a small smile. Mrs. Nell, her gaze still fixed on him, reached for the phone and dialed. "Hi, sweetheart, it's Mom. I need you to come home right away," she said into the receiver. "Is everything alright?" Nado asked, concern evident in his voice. Mrs. Nell paused before replying, "Everything's fine, dear. Just come as soon as you can." After hearing Nado's reassurance that he'd be there shortly, she hung up. Now, all there was left to do was wait and see how the situation would unfold.

"May I get you a drink, Dan?" Mrs. Nell offered. With an appreciative nod, Dan accepted. Retreating to the kitchen, Mrs. Nell's hand instinctively reached for the small bottle of concentrated lemonade in the fridge. Dan had always loved her homemade lemonade. She wondered if he still did. Preparing it as she used to and garnishing it with a fresh lemon slice, she returned to the den and handed Dan the glass.

The familiar taste sparked a rush of memories, moving Dan to tears. "You've remembered my favorite after all these years," Dan managed to say, wiping away his tears. Mrs. Nell yearned to console him but hesitated, the pain he had once caused her holding her back.

Lost in thought, Mrs. Nell was startled by the sudden entrance of Nado. His gaze landed instantly on 2-4. At that moment, Nado faced a difficult choice - let his pride intervene or embrace 2-4 as his father.

Before Nado could make a move, 2-4 returned the lemonade to Mrs. Nell and stepped up to Nado. A tense silence filled the room, broken briefly by simultaneous, confused attempts at conversation. Then, silence reigned again, ultimately giving way to a heartfelt embrace. Their first.

Words were unnecessary; the intensity of their hug spoke volumes. Their shared tears of joy signaled a mutual understanding - they needed each other. Today was indeed special.

"I once fled from my mistakes. I can't repeat that," said 2-4, looking at Nado. "When I saw you on TV, your final words felt like they were meant for me."

Nado smiled back. "My words were meant to inspire all absentee fathers. But I was also reaching out to you, the father I never knew. We all err, but what matters is how we make amends." He noticed 2-4's quizzical expression. "What about your sister?" 2-4 asked. Nado countered with his own question, "Did you ask mom about me?"

"No, she likely wouldn't have told me," 2-4 admitted.

"Do you understand why?" Nado pressed.

"I suppose so," 2-4 confessed.

Nado, however, was unsatisfied with his father's guesswork. "No more guessing. Mom couldn't predict my reactions to you, just like we can't predict Necy's. You need to experience fatherhood firsthand. Shall we go see her?" Nado proposed. They shared a laugh, promising Mrs. Nell they'd return, and as they left, Dan made a request, "Save that lemonade for me. It's as good as I remember."

Watching her son and his estranged father drive off, Mrs. Nell reflected on her feelings towards Dan. She'd believed she harbored hatred for him, but now, confronting him, she realized it was more resentment. The abandonment and the burden of raising two children alone had left her yearning for answers. Now that she had them, she felt a weight lift.

Snapped from her daydream by a passing car's horn, she returned inside, pondering her next steps. She knew she needed to be patient. Maybe, just maybe, the family she'd always wanted was within reach. Spotting the lemonade on the table, she smiled, just like the old days.

THE END

9 798988 530367